Contents

Dear Reader

...or shall I call you **adventurer**?

This latter might be more accurate, as this book is nothing like a traditional one — this book is your story. You are in the middle of the happenings, and you can and will shape the story by your decisions.

Of course, within the book's limits, but that is still giving you an awful lot of chances to make the right call — or make the wrong ones too!

For achieving that, you should not read the following chapters in order as they appear on the pages, but rather you'd have to make a call or decision after every smaller or bigger chapter and decide in which direction you'd like to go. Then turn to the referred chapter and carry on reading to get a coherent story.

If a chapter does not have any indication what to do, that means you reached a dead-end in the story, where you cannot recover from — that means you'd need to start over.

But let's not talk about failures. Let's talk about success and fun.

That you can engage with the entire story, you can get used to making decisions, making tough calls, some challenging ones sometimes. But, I feel it important to mention that this book is going to challenge your critical thinking and wittiness. It can be humorous and sad at some points but, most importantly, its main goal is to entertain you, opening up a new world for you that exists only on books' pages.

In this story, you are going to discover some aspect of an ancient world that has a lot of similarities with our world.

I wrote this book as a birthday present for my best friend for life, as a reminder that we had been kids sometime and tried to make him nostalgic about childhood, romanticize that era, and bring back fond memories that had never been forgotten in time.

I really like to greet him here as I did in the manuscript when I gave it to him, so the next section is for him.

As for you, my dear reader, my dear adventurer, please read through the instructions and rules before you start with the first chapter.

Good luck!

My Dearest Friend

📖 Foreword

Welcome to this old-new adventure!

You surely remember how enthusiastically we used to write You Are The Hero-style stories at the bus stop, exclaiming "I'll catch the next one" when we saw the bus turning the corner too son; well, looking back at this defining period of my life has led me to the point where, even after all these years, I return to that old-fashioned fun and write such a story again, especially for you — to give your brain a little workout if everyday life hasn't done so enough.

Well.

Since I have just revealed that the target audience of this adventure I created is specifically you, I assume I don't need to introduce the narrative structure, nor explain why, from where, and to where you need to turn at certain points in the story, as (in theory) the flow of the story does not differ in any way from those ingrained in our in-stincts.

At the same time, I tried to incorporate some extra creative elements, without overcomplicating the setup and the administration, making the survival and the gameplay more interesting instead. I can reveal in advance that every detail may be important at later points in the story, and naturally, not every path leads to certain death in the nar-rative[1], as matter of fact there is a lot of opportunity to recover and continue the story. The story also received a proper ending (I hope!), as it should.

However, I consider it important to mention that I created this story in the old traditional way: with paper, eraser, pencil, and I also made a proper map of the world of Vilia, in a small corner of which this story

---

[1] We had enjoyed developing stories that often ended in the "death" of the player, just as a courtesy of an everlasting friendship.

takes place. I wanted to add some small puzzles as well to make the final result somewhat authentic.

So, I won't elaborate too much on the original turn-the-page-and-continue-at principle. As the story requires, you'll naturally need to flip to the continuation depending on how you'd decide (or are able to decide) in the given situation regarding the current circumstances. Each such jump-to-the-next-chapter is indicated by a specific number, something like this: #1234 (if all goes well and you have the digital version of the book, clicking on the number will automatically shift the focus to the designated chapter without you worrying for a blink of an eye).

I will use pictograms in many places, which will always mean the same thing, simply out of laziness, it's easier and simpler than typing (I hope the idea will be more useful than annoying).

🏛 The basic mechanics

What you'd need...

...is a sheet of 📄 paper, ✏ pencil, ◇ eraser, and ideally two **(D6)** 🎲 dice. Of course, a little spare time to delve into the story.

If you fancy drawing a map of your journey, well, then a "little" bit more paper.

You can play this book on two different difficulties.

The **normal** difficulty is when you use and roll the dice, and live through all the tension of the combat, or when you'd need to use your dexterity or luck, and deal with the consequences.

The **easy** difficulty is when you can skip all the dice-rolling and just assume that you win all the fights and you get lucky every time, and assume every challenging scenario is resolved in your favor, and you can enjoy the storyline and its challenging puzzles.

> I recommend to read through all the rules.

However, you can download the mobile app from my website, just scan the QR code to open it on your mobile. The mobile app simplifies managing the character's attributes, keeping your inventory up to date, and has the entire combat  mechanism. The app lets you keep the main focus on the storyline, rather than requiring you to keep all rules in mind while reading.

The Story and the Universe

The story itself was inspired by multiple sources; it's essentially fantasy, but I definitely — even if unintentionally — drew a lot from the good old books we used to read back in the day.

The world we are playing is called Vilia, and it is basically covered by huge kingdoms that are, of course, in some kind of disagreement or even at war with each other. That is you to find out as the story goes. It is not a secret but I would not like to spoil the story, it might give you some tension and chill at some point.

In this world, you need to navigate your character from the beginning to the end of the story.

I will try to mark the names of cities or notable places of the map in the text with a 🗺**map**, so you know these are places you might be able to visit as your adventure goes.

The game will require you to carefully note down (or simply remember) several things. I won't reveal in the text which details are important or not, only where and how you can use certain information at specific places (if you have it). You need to figure out where to get that information, or how to move forward without it. So, it is worth paying attention to this, as several chapters of the story can only be accessed this way — and often, you might get stuck in the story because you lack some piece of information.

It could be that you have not discovered yet, and you need to come back to that place, or it is possible that you have already encountered the information, but you simply missed it out, as it was not important.

So, at certain points in the story, you'll need to do a bit of thinking to find or discover things that are only accessible with prior information, a trick, or the use of an item. I will clearly mark these moments in the story with a 💡**lightbulb**, so you know there's something you might or must use, and I'll also describe there how you can do that. If you have the necessary information or item, it will be easy to follow the instructions and continue the story along that path, if you don't have that, the instructions probably will mean nothing to you. You may need a calculator for that do quickly the additions or subtractions, based on the instructions.

Your Character

You create your own character. The book does not tell you about this character's gender, age, or religion, that is all up to you to build up your persona who you'd like to play the game with.

It makes no difference at all, as every character has the same properties during the journey but it is up to your imagination whether your player is supposed to masculine or feminine, tall or short, or young or old. That is where your imagination begins.

To start, your character has nothing, not even gold coins (⊛). However, this is an important currency in the game; you can buy many things with it, and of course, the shiny metal can also be the source of a few other conflicts you may encounter.

At the same time, your character has two important attributes.

1. Your ⚡**HEALTH**. You can determine the starting value by rolling a die (⚃) and adding 6 to the value.

2. Your 〰**SKILL** or 〰**DEXTERITY**. You can determine the starting value by rolling a die, (⚃) dividing the result by 2, and using the number shown (If it's odd, round up to the nearest whole freely, e.g. you roll 5, then dividing it by 2 leads you to 2.5 which is 3 after rounding it up).

In the game, you will find ⚡-boosting potions or foods, which you can carry in unlimited numbers and consume at any time (even during a combat). Health points can freely exceed the original starting value at any time, meaning you can become stronger than you were at the start.

The 〰 points can only be increased when the story provides an opportunity for it, which can happen in various ways: through reading, practicing, learning, or even after a tough battle.

Items and Objects

Items that can be picked up will be marked in the text with 🧺**basket** before their names. These are items you can possess or carry with you to use later (or not, haha, you'll only find out afterward which was handy or not).

There's no limit to how many items you can carry.

There are various types of items in the game.

The first type is the ordinary item, they don't have any, this kind of item can be consumable, – edible, drinkable, – and gives extra ⚡**HEALTH** or ⚎**STRENGTH** points once you consume it. There is no special time or moment when you can consume these items. Feel free to eat an apple even during the combat, if your health is low.

The second type of items are the wearable items, they are marked by ⚎ as they could give extra advantage during the fight, increase your – or decrease – your opponents ⚡**HEALTH**, 〰**DEXTERITY**, or overall ⓪─⓪STRENGTH that you are welcome to use during any combat scenarios.

If you acquire items or tools that have additional effects on your combat abilities, specifically on calculated ⓪─⓪STRENGTH points, e.g., **+2**⓪─⓪STRENGTH, you can automatically use them during combat as long as you have the item (no worries, I'll explain ⓪─⓪STRENGTH points and combat in the next chapter). There may also be items, mostly magical ones (or weapons), that don't increase your own ⓪─⓪STRENGTH points but reduce the opponent's during combat.

I won't emphasize this in the text or during the game, but I consider it obvious that, just as you can't normally wear 10 pairs of gloves, 5 helmets, or 3 sets of armors, you can't do so in the game either.

You can only use one item of each type when calculating your ⓪─⓪STRENGTH points before combat.

The and third – and last – type of item is the weapon, they are marked with the →|← symbol, and they are the ones that can cause significant damage to your opponents, and win a fight or battle with.

If you sell, give away, trade, lost, drop, or have any item stolen from you, you can no longer use it – just remove it from your item list.

🏃 The Combat

Damage and Shield

There will be opponents and enemies in the game, those could be regular creatures, animals, or in this story you can encounter supernatural creatures, such as ghosts or living skeletons too. These may give you some goosebumps, but they won't do too much to you beyond the fact that you have to fight with them following the rules of the game.

Let's see how simple the combat is, despite the seemingly convoluted description.

Every weapon has a →|← DAMAGE and a 🛡SHIELD point.

A weapon's →|← and 🛡 points written like 3→|←5🛡, where **3** is the →|← DAMAGE point and **5** is the 🛡SHIELD strength.

Every weapon look like that. Your opponents will have the same values of their current weapon, which makes them either a laughing matter or deadly threat.

When you encounter a weapon and decided to carry, write down these numbers next to weapon in your inventory, as you'll need them during every combat, right immediately when calculating your 🏋STRENGTH points before the fight.

You need to calculate first your and your opponent's 🏋 points independently:

1. Your 🏋 = (your 🏋 + your weapon's →|← - opponent's 🛡) ± additional 🏋

2. Opponent 🏋 = (opponent 🏋 + their weapon's →|← - your 🛡) ± additional 🏋

Note the extra additional 🏋 value at the end of the lines, that means if you have an item, an enchanted weapon, or anything that directly increase your points or or decrease your opponent's points, than you have to apply those here. If an item in your possession has a positive extra 🏋STRENGTH point that means it increases your strength, if the value is negative it reduces your opponent's 🏋STRENGTH points. Same applies on the way around, if your opponent has a enchanted item with additional positive extra 🏋STRENGTH points, that increases their strength, while if they have a negative 🏋STRENGTH point, that will reduce yours in the combat.

So, bear in mind, your opponent could have and might have similar additional advantage against you! If that is the case and they have such a weapon in their possession, it will be clearly stated in the description.

These 🏋STRENGTH values will act like indicators of how strong the parties compared to each other, and the comparison is simple as:

Your ⚔	Opponent ⚔	Result
0 or less	0 or less	Neither of you is strong enough to defeat the other. **You will both flee** from each other, **unharmed**, and the battle will end.
0 or less	1 or greater	Your opponent is stronger, and you'd better flee. **Your opponent deals one hit to you**, and you must reduce your ⚡ points by your opponent's ⚔ value. It may also happen that they fatally wound you while fleeing, in which case your character suffers sudden death.
1 or greater	0 or less	You are stronger than your opponent, who will naturally try to flee. However, you deal one hit to them, and you must reduce their ⚡ points by your own ⚔ value. It may also happen that you fatally wound them while they flee, in which case your opponent dies immediately, and you can enjoy all the benefits of this.
1 or greater	1 or greater	In this case both of you are strong enough to harm each other, and **there will be a real fight between you** as per described below.

After calculating your own and your opponents' ⚔ points, you can already see roughly your chances of winning the battle, if you decide to engage.

Naturally, if you have another type of weapon that you can use with higher ⚔ points, fell free to recalculate your and your opponent's points to see how much your chances have changed. Alternatively, you can flee without fighting, but if it's your opponent's turn to attack next, they will try to deal one hit to you while you flee, and you must take that damage.

Generally, if it's your turn to attack, fleeing has no consequences. You can also flee at any time during the battle if the ground starts feeling too hot under your feet and you can no longer use more ⚡-boosting potions or foods, but if you can fell free to apply them anytime for surviving the combat!

The Various Weapons

To accurately outline the course of combat, I first need to mention a few things about the weapons used in the game.

I've categorized the weapons in the game into three types, and accordingly, I've developed three different combat modes. These combat modes apply to both you and your opponent, depending on what type of weapon you use to attack each other.

It is not too complicated as these modes are based on real-life mechanics as well, so it will be easy to remember. If you are unsure about these, just turn the page over and read this again, even during the battle.

No weapon type has an advantage or disadvantage over another; each type can realistically defeat any other type, but your character's style might prefer one to another for various reasons.

◎ Bows and Arrows

Pros	Cons
The number of arrows is unlimited.	Low 🛡 value.
You can find special or strong arrows (however, their number is limited).	
You can start the combat with 3 consequent rounds of attacking before your opponent could engage.	

With a bow, you can primarily take down your opponents from a distance, which is why the one who starts the attack gets the opportunity for 3 consequent shots at the beginning of the battle. Usually you have the opportunity to attack first, but don't forget, if your opponent uses a bow and arrows, they also get the chance for 3 consecutive shots, if the game specifically states that they can attack first, rather than you!

⊙ Swords and Shields

Pros	Cons
Exceptionally high 🛡 value.	It won't affect the standard combat mechanics in any way.
Exceptionally high →|← value.	
They could be enchanted which decreases the opponent's ⚊ points.	

The swords and shields are traditional equipment and do not guarantee any special advantages during the combat.

◯ Knives and Daggers

Pros	Cons
After a successful attack, it can attack again immediately.	Low →|← value.
Guarantee to be able to attack first.	
They could be enchanted which decreases the opponent's ◑═◐ points.	

Knives and daggers are primarily close-combat weapons with low damage values, but when you attack with them, it always guarantees that the first round is yours. If your opponent also attacks with knives and daggers, you will get the first round. Even if your opponent attacks with a bow and arrows and would normally get the first 3 rounds, you can still attack first, and your opponent cannot shoot at you 3 times.

Animals or Other living beings

In the game, there are creatures (flora and fauna, marked with 🔥 fire) that do not have weapons and have no privileges against your chosen weapon.

However, they still have ⚡HEALTH, →\|←DAMAGE, and 🛡SHIELD points, which are necessary for calculating the ◑═◐STRENGTH values for the combat.

These creatures do not have any 🗲SKILL or 🗲DEXTERITY points (consider these values as zero for the calculations we talked about earlier).

However, their →\|←DAMAGE value can be quite high. For example, an average bear has 25⚡🔥12→\|←8🛡 points, while a common hare has 4⚡🔥2→\|←3🛡.

Combat with them can be quite varied, even though they can always attack for one round (whether successful or not), while you can use the advantages of your chosen weapon against them as well.

Fighting multiple enemies simultaneously

It will happen several times that you have to face multiple enemies at once (I'll mostly throw you into the deep end of this). These situations are essentially handled like in old action movies: only one enemy attacks you at a time, while the others just hover around cluelessly waiting for their turn to attack you, that gives you the great advantage to fight the opponents one by one.

If multiple enemies appear at once, I will leave it to you to decide the order in which you fight them.

You have one advantage: in such cases, if you deliver a fatal hit to one enemy, the next round is yours again, and you can use all the advantages of your weapon against the next enemy as if it were the first round of the attack, regardless of what weapon the next enemy uses against you.

You might face a long combat, but you have a healthy situation in your hand to defeat all of them. Luck may not be with you all the time, but that is why it is called luck.

The actual fight!

As you can see, different weapon types result in different combat dynamics.

Before starting a fight, you must choose which weapon type you'll use to attack your opponent (especially if you have multiple weapons).

You cannot change this weapon during that fight. You can choose a different weapons for each opponent, but after your choice is made you have to conduct the fight with that weapon of your choice.

The combat proceeds as follows: if both your and your opponent's **STRENGTH** values are positive, you take turns attacking each other, trying to defeat one another. If you are not happy with the calculated points, you can recalculate them with different weapons to see whether that improves your chance of winning.

Depending on the weapons used, the combat may have custom mechanics based on the weapon's properties; keep that in mind as a wisely chosen weapon might give you just the right advantage to get glorious!

Generally, unless the game specifies otherwise, you get the first round of attack.

How can you tell if your weapon has damaged your opponent, or if your opponent has damaged you?

This is determined by the previously calculated **STRENGTH** points and the ⚃ die roll[2]: if the rolled value is greater than the attacker's **STRENGTH** points, the attack deals damage; if not, the other party blocks the attack, no damage was done[3].

You might need to use multiple dice, or roll one more than once to determine the rolled value properly. Here a simple table which tells you how many rolls you need to do and summarize the value to determine the success of the attach.

---

[2] You need to roll the dice for your opponent too.

[3] In the mobile app that works slightly more balanced, there is always a 50-50 chance to strike successfully or block a strike.

Attacker's 💪	Number of Dice Rolls
Between **1** and **5**	🎲
Between **6** and **11**	🎲 🎲
Between **12** and **17**	🎲 🎲 🎲
Between **18** and **23**	🎲 🎲 🎲 🎲
Between **24** and **29**	🎲 🎲 🎲 🎲 🎲
Between **30** and **35**	🎲 🎲 🎲 🎲 🎲 🎲
And so on...	

In practice, you'll see that this approach balances the combat by increasing the number of dice rolls to give you a great chance of defeating much stronger opponents than yourself. It's easy to notice that if one party, for example, can deal damage with **20 💪 STRENGTH** points, they could easily finish off their opponent, possibly in a single round. If you are the winner that would be in your favor, however you can be on the other side of the history which gives every opponent a fair chance to win any kind of fight.

If the attack is successful, you must reduce the damaged party's **⚡HEALTH** points by the attacker's **💪STRENGTH** points. If the **⚡HEALTH** points of any party drops to zero or below, that means the party is considered dead.

It is better to see some example, just in case.

Examples of combat

Let's say you're well into the adventure with **14⚡** and **5🌱** points, and you have a nifty little sword and shield, such as **8→|←5🛡**.

Your opponent is currently a bit weaker than you: **11⚡** and **3🌱** points, but they're coming at you with a magical knife and dagger

3→|←2⚔-3⛨, which has the magical property of reducing the opponent's – in this case, your – ⛨STRENGTH points by 3.

Once again: if a weapon's properties include negative ⛨STRENGTH points, those are always subtracted from the opponent's points; if the value is positive, it's taken into account and added to when calculating the ⛨STRENGTH points of the person using the weapon.

You can do a quick calculation: when both of your ⛨STRENGTH values are positive, despite your reduced ⛨STRENGTH points you can still deal massive hit to your opponent, so let the example battle begin!

Your opponent attacks with knives and daggers, so they get the first round of attack and can keep attacking as long as they can deal damage, in this case thanks to you strong shield the damage is only negligible.

Let's follow the combat as per the rules of the game.

Round	You with Swords (14⚡5🌀8→|←5🛡)	⚡	Opponent with Daggers (11⚡3🌀3→|←2🛡-3⚙)	⚡
0th	+5🌀+8→|←-2🛡-3⚙ = 8⚙	14	+3🌀+3→|←-5🛡 = 1⚙	11
1st		13	🎲(4), **4 > 1,** (-1⚡ from you)	11
2nd		12	🎲(5), **5 > 1,** (-1⚡ from you)	11
3rd		11	🎲(2), **2 > 1,** (-1⚡ from you)	11
4th		11	🎲(1), **1 = 1,** (✗ missed you)	11
5th	🎲🎲(10), **10 > 8,** (-8⚡ from them)	11		3
6th		10	🎲(4), **2 > 1,** (-1⚡ from you)	3
7th		9	🎲(3), **3 > 1,** (-1⚡ from you)	3
8th		9	🎲(1), **1 = 1,** (✗ missed you)	3
9th	🎲🎲(9), **9 > 8,** (-8⚡ from them)	9	🏵 (defeated)	0

This is a risky battle, but since your opponent has only **1⚙STRENGTH**, that basically gave you a great change to win the bottle, as you can see your opponent hit you 5 times, while you hit them only 2 times to nullify their ⚡**HEALTH**. Okay, you suffered damage but the changes of you winning it was much greater.

Let's see what happens when you face the same opponent, but you're using knives and daggers, while they wield a sword and shield!

This means you'll need to reduce your opponent's **STRENGTH** points by 3 during the calculation, so your **STRENGTH** points will look a bit different now.

It's clear that your opponent can bring quite a damage to you now, but you have the initiative since the first round is yours due to your chosen weapon, and you can attack continuously until you miss a round.

Round	You with Daggers (14⚡5⚗3→|←2🛡-3⚙)	⚡	Opponent with Swords (11⚡3⚗8→|←5🛡)	⚡
0th	+5⚗+3→|←-5🛡 = 3⚙	14	+3⚗+8→|←-2🛡-3⚙ = 6⚙	11
1st	🎲(4), **4 > 3**, (-3⚡ from them)	14		8
2nd	🎲(6), **6 > 3**, (-3⚡ from them)	14		5
3rd	🎲(2), **2 < 3**, (✕ missed them)	14		5
4th		8	🎲🎲(9), **10 > 8**, (-6⚡ from you)	5
5th	🎲(5), **5 > 3**, (-3⚡ from them)	8		2
6th	🎲(1), **1 < 3**, (✕ missed them)	8		2
7th		8	🎲🎲(6), **6 = 6**, (✕ missed you)	2
8th	🎲(6), **6 > 3**, (-3⚡ from them)	8	⚰ (defeated)	0

Well, that's how the combat might've played out after a few simple calculations and dice rolls when the weapons are swapped.

You can see now the combat is quite simple, it may take a few rounds but eventually your wise choices can lead you to victory.

It's important to know that you can eat or drink at any time during combat, which can increase your ⚡**HEALTH** points, while your opponents will never be able to do such a thing, and it's definitely worth taking advantage of this during a fight.

I reckon you are just ready to start.

The Story

📖 Once upon a time...

For thirteen days and twelve nights, you drifted on the sea in this small fishing boat, and every part of you was completely frozen by the time you finally caught sight of the outlines of land on the horizon. You sighed with relief, knowing that soon you would feel solid ground beneath your feet again – and you don't have to endure this stinky fish smell any longer.

As the sturdy wooden vessel glided gracefully toward the bustling port, the radiant sun cast golden shards across the rippling azure waves, dancing like scattered jewels upon the sea. The salt-kissed breeze carried the faint, earthy aromas of distant lands, mingling with the spicy tang of the ocean air. Billowing clouds, soft and alabaster, floated lazily against a cerulean canvas, their shadows painting fleeting patterns on the water's shimmering surface. Along the rugged coastline, towering stone walls and crimson-tiled rooftops basked under the warm glow, their reflections winking like ancient secrets in the gentle tide. Seagulls wheeled overhead, their jubilant cries harmonizing with the rhythmic creak of timbers and the lapping of waves, heralding the approach of adventure and the timeless embrace of the storied harbor ahead.

The boat is getting closer to the pier, and so are you, to finally meeting Kiena. She might be able to help you find the lost stones, or at least one of them.

Captain Davismore was a good man, he kept everyone disciplined during the journey but treated the crew, you, and your five companions with fairness. Naturally, this was to be expected; you wanted to repay the captain's compassion, the voyage, the food, the hospitality, and simply the fact that he took you on, through hard work. Overall, you can sit back satisfied, as you will be docking with rich loot at the port of 📖 **Dispel** – which was your destination after all. This was the agreement you made with Captain Davismore: he would bring you here, and you would repay him with honest work — since unfortunately you had no gold left when you met him during your adventures.

So it's already certain that you'll need to find some work at the port to buy bread, and you'll also need to secure some lodging to stay while you figure out where to go from here. Kiena would be the next stop on your journey, but aside from the fact that she was last seen somewhere in the 📖 **Mudwodian Empire**, there isn't much information about where to look for her.

Perhaps you can ask around at the local tavern. That is probably your best bet.

You lean over the side of the boat, scanning the approaching shore. The unpleasant, screeching song of the seagulls has etched itself into your ears over the past few days, as they have followed the ship all along, no doubt in hopes of snagging something for themselves. Whatever the case, they've become almost a part of your days, and now you would hear them for a while, even if not a single one were circling around the boat.

However, this day was not so fortunate; more and more circulated in the air as the harbor approached. You are getting ready to perform your last duty on this boat.

The docking went smoothly; the waves didn't rock the boat much this time. You helped secure the ropes, and once the boat was firmly tied to the dock, you approached Captain Davismore to thank him for his help and for bringing you this far. It's clear that your paths will diverge from here, but you don't want to burn this bridge behind you — you might need his help again someday.

Captain Davismore was grateful that you helped him return with a fully loaded ship, the richly loaded ship promises a good profit for him. As a token of his gratitude, he gives you a 🧺 **large basket of fish**, which you might be able to sell at the fish market for some gold, enough to afford a warm soup somewhere and continue your journey.

You shake hands and thank him for the journey. Captain Davismore tells you that they will be at the port for a few more days, in case you need anything – you might be able to help each other again.

Continue at #1.

#1

You are standing at the harbor. In the distance, you see the city walls along with the towering spires reaching into the sky. After a few brief inquiries and conversations with the locals, it quickly becomes clear that the fastest way to the downtown area from here is through the Wamake Gate (#140), from where an even more direct road leads to the Citadel.

There is a blacksmith shop (#220) outside the city, Youngrek is the local blacksmith here, he is an ogre but very friendly according to the locals, so, it might be worth talking to him. The large marketplace (#181) is just a few streets away from here, where you can surely buy food and clothes.

To the fish market (#320), you don't even have to walk more than three steps, and there you can buy and sell as much fish as you aren't ashamed of.

If you would like to leave the city on a departing ship, you can also speak with the captains (#49).

#2

The chest is completely empty.

You can try to open the iron-barred gate (#245).

You can start exploring the corridor (#152).

You can climb back through the narrow and damp tunnel you came through (#33).

#3

You enter a small chamber where the entire northern corner is submerged in water. There appear to be no other exits from the room, and as you step inside, a skeleton in the eastern corner emerged and slowly comes to life to confront you.

Skeleton (with a Sword)　　　　18⚡5🗡 ⊙6→|←2🛡

If you successfully defeat the skeleton, you can look around the chamber a bit more (#258), or if you've seen enough, you can leave the room the way you came (#376).

#4

Stumbling along the corridor, you come across a T-shaped junction.

> The mud reaches up to your knees, making it very difficult and unsteady to move forward. You slip and stumble, barely managing to keep your balance.
>
> Roll two dice, and if the resulting number is greater than your 🗡 points, deduct **-1⚡** from yourself as you trip in the mud, fall, and suffer a minor injury.

To the right, the corridor continues, but you can't quite make out where it leads (#353).

Straight ahead, a larger chamber looms in front of you (#378).

The third branch of the junction leads toward some kind of staircase (#121).

#5

The city tavern is bustling with life, though most of the patrons are shady-looking characters. They seem harmless enough, laughing, feasting, and drinking, with no one looking for trouble.

You can examine the people inside to see if you notice anything interesting (#395).

If none of them catch your fancy, you can sit at one of the empty tables alone (#109).

Or, as a last resort, you can strike up a conversation with the bartender (#281).

If you've seen enough of the tavern, you can head back to the main square (#348).

#6

You stand in the middle of the marketplace, where there's quite a bustle for the size of the village. People are haggling, buying, and selling, and you can find a wide variety of things here.

You might even be able to sell something if you feel like it.

If you have a 🧺**large basket of fish**, you can try to sell it here for **6**✹.

If you have a 🧺**shovel**, you can try to sell it here for **3**✹.

If you have a 🧺**rasp**, you can try to sell it here for **2**✹.

If you have a 🧺**whetstone**, you can try to sell it here for **1**✹.

On the other side of the marketplace is the village tavern, which you can check out (#203).

The main street continues at the far corner of the marketplace and seems to lead toward the mill (#122).

If you'd like to return to 📖 **Dispel**, you can do that as well (#157).

#7

You reach for the bluish flowers and grab them; the blue light emanating from the altar doesn't stop you.

With the 🗑blue flowers (84-7) in your hand, it's time to respectfully step away from the altar (#71).

#8

This part of the passage seems to have collapsed on its own over time, perhaps because the tunnel's ceiling wasn't strong enough and likely gave way under its own weight. After a first glance, you're optimistic that with some effort, you can clear the path. You start moving the stones out of the way, one after another.

It feels like an endless task to clear the tunnel and remove the stones from the path. You become thoroughly exhausted, and by the time you realize this will take much more time and determination, you're panting and leaning against the wall. Due to the fatigue, you lose **-1⚡** point.

If you haven't already, you can examine the fountain more closely (#65).

Or, heading south past the broken iron bars, you can crawl through the increasingly narrow tunnel (#163).

#9

A short walk along the path through the park leads you straight to the riverbank, which is almost more pleasant and peaceful than the central part of the park. Yellow flowers cover everything here as well, arranged in neat little beds. As far as you can see, no one is around right now.

There's not much to see on the riverbank; a few large willow trees hang their branches obediently, casting shade over nearly the entire riverbank, where benches have been placed for the comfort of visitors.

It might not be entirely proper, but if you wish, you can take 🧺**a few yellow flowers (5-42)** with you; they have a pleasant fragrance. If you carry them, these sweet-smelling yellow flowers grant you **+1** 🍃 point as long as you have them.

From here, you can easily walk back along the small path to the park (#276).

#10

Several keys hang on the wall, hooked onto a ring, some of them quite rusted, but upon closer inspection, you see that each key is identical, at least based on their teeth. You're not sure why so many duplicates are needed, but if you'd like, you can take a 🧺**cell key (1-9)** with you, as it might come in handy later.

There's not much else to see here.

From here, you can head toward the cells via the southeastern branch of the corridor (#280).

Or, there are two other exits from the room: a long, narrow corridor leads northwest (#288), and through a smaller passage to the northeast, you can see another larger chamber (#376).

#11

When you inquire about his activities, he responds with a confident glint in his eye, declaring that he's the sole mage in the region skilled enough to concoct potions for any ailment or predicament. The townsfolk hold him in high esteem, appreciating his rare talents, yet the bustling city life holds no charm for him. Instead, he finds solace in this serene riverside haven, where the gentle murmur of flowing water and the whispering breeze through the reeds soothe his spirit. From this tranquil spot, he can effortlessly venture into the lush, emerald forests nearby, gathering fragrant herbs and rare botanicals for his magical brews.

He has a few interesting items in his inventory for a warrior like you, if you're willing to part with some gold.

You can buy a 🧺 ᴑ⊨ᴑ **stamina potion** from him, which you can use in one combat only to instantly gain **+20**⚡ points, for **20**✷, if you possess that much.

You can buy a 🧺 ᴑ⊨ᴑ **combat potion** from him, which you can use in one combat only to instantly deal **-50**⚡ damage to all current enemies (no matter how many you're fighting), for **25**✷, if you possess that much.

You can buy a 🧺 ᴑ⊨ᴑ **protective potion** from him, which you can use once to instantly gain **+10**🛡 points for the duration of the current battle, for **15**✷, if you possess that much.

Of course, you're not obligated to buy anything from him. You could ask about Kiena; he might know something (#273), or you could inquire about the commotion with the guarded city gates (#151), if you haven't already.

After a friendly goodbye, you can continue your journey along the path between the houses to the north (#39) or follow the city wall to the west (#238).

#12

You travel along the road for a while until you reach a junction.

More precisely, a crossroads, as you could head back along the wide road toward 🔖**Dispel**, but it would be a waste to retrace that long journey now — the signpost points to equally intriguing places, and Kiena can't be too far away.

To the west, you can follow the narrower crossroad toward 🔖**Moonward** (#106).

To the southeast, another branch of the narrow crossroad leads toward 🔖**Ugmarltyher** (#84).

To the south, the wide road continues toward 🔖**Dig** (#244). From what you've heard about this place, it's well beyond the empire's borders, the capital of the Mokro Kingdom, about 900 miles from here. Hopefully, you won't need to go that far.

#13

Someone has heard your sneaky noises and hurries toward the ground floor with quick steps. You take advantage of the loud sound of their hurried footsteps and swiftly leave the house through the same way you entered, before anyone truly notices you were there.

Either way, deduct **-1**🦡 point from yourself for your clumsiness.

You make your way back through the surrounding streets toward the main road, breathing a sigh of relief that you escaped without any unpleasant consequences (#169).

#14

Bukatzi bursts out laughing at your question, his eyes gleaming with a mischief that hints at secrets untold. It's as though he's privy to the hidden currents swirling beneath the surface of mundane chatter. Leaning in with a conspiratorial grin, he recounts a snippet he over-heard — a hushed, electrified whisper from a shadowy corner of the tavern, plotting a daring heist against the Citadel's formidable stronghold. But Bukatzi waves it off with a theatrical shrug; schemes like these drift through the air as commonly as the scent of spiced ale. The Citadel, a fortress cradling untold riches, lures dreamers and desperados alike. To Bukatzi, hearing of such reckless ambition is as routine as the sunrise — yet each tale carries the tantalizing thrill of what might just be the one audacious enough to succeed.

You ask which table he overheard this at, and the bartender nods to-ward a table by one of the windows. Three people are sitting there, and it's easy to remember because it's right next to a pillar where someone carved three clearly readable numbers under a stag's antlers: 24-4.

You can ask what they're celebrating here (#190).

You can press him for local gossip (#117).

Or, if you're done questioning the bartender, you can sit at a quiet ta-ble where someone is already slumped over, fast asleep (#212), or join someone at another table who's peacefully sipping from their mug (#337).

#15

You sprint down a narrow street. To your right, you see the city wall. The scent of the salty sea hits your nose from somewhere nearby.

The guards are hot on your heels.

You can go right (#346), forward (#358), or left (#310).

#16

Elliniar warmly greets you as he sees you again, wiping his forehead as he pauses for a moment from his intense work. You notice he's still diligently working on the spears. From what you can see, he's making good progress — there are several new spears in the weapon rack compared to the last time you were here (#162).

#17

You walk into a small chamber that is completely empty, with no signs indicating what it might have been used for in its prime.

What is certain is that the chamber has three exits.

You can head southeast along a narrower corridor (#288).

To the west, another corridor leads onward, though you can't quite see its end, but you can go that way too (#277).

Or, to the northwest, a path leads through a door to another chamber where you can make out an altar in the distance (#365).

#18

You tell Oreth you'd like to rest at his place if he has a free room for a weary traveler like yourself. Oreth says he has two rooms, both currently available, so you're in luck if you want to stay.

You can pay **8**⊛ for a room (#126).

Or you can ask him about Kiena, in case he knows something about her (#76).

You can inquire about the local wine (#357).

You can sit at an empty table and order something to eat or drink (#109).

You can ask about the reasons for the increased guard presence (#200).

You can look around the tavern and check out the people drinking here (#395).

Or you can leave the tavern and head back to the main square (#348).

#19

You step into the bustling workshop, where the rhythmic clatter of tools fills the air, mingling with the sharp scent of freshly cut wood. Dust motes dance in the golden shafts of sunlight streaming through the high windows. Amidst the controlled chaos, a burly, bearded man strains to hoist an enormous log onto a sturdy saw-bench. His muscles ripple under the strain, veins bulging, his face flushed and glistening with sweat. The sheer size of the log makes you wonder how he managed to drag it this far, a feat that seems as impressive as it is improbable. Each labored breath he takes adds to the palpable tension, a silent testament to his grit and determination.

You greet him, and the craftsman pauses, wiping his forehead, clearly grateful for a moment's rest.

"Greetings, stranger! What brings you here?" he calls out loudly.

You return the greeting and learn his name is Ifer, the local carpenter and woodcutter. He explains he's currently working on building a cabinet but is struggling with the task, as his apprentice is still out in the forest working.

It's clear he could use some help (#292), and you might earn a few gold coins by assisting him.

If you don't want to help, you can ask him about 📖 **Dispel** (#328).

Or, if you feel there's nothing for you here, you can walk back out to the street (#77).

#20

The road leads straight to the city gate, where the guards vigilantly watch who comes and goes. The gate is a bit dilapidated on the outside, having seen better days, but it could probably still withstand a small siege if it came to that.

You can try to walk past the guards and enter the city (#161).

If you have a 💡**vial of essential oil**, you can use it here by multiplying the two numbers, adding the result to this chapter's number, and continuing your reading there.

Alternatively, you can head south along a narrower path between the houses, following the city wall (#356).

Or you can follow the road east back toward the bridge (#39).

#21

If this is the first time you're examining the stone slab (#111), or if you've already done so before (#371).

#22

You hear loud shouting; the sounds of the battle didn't go unnoticed. Three more guards rush toward you from the city to avenge your massacre. Either way, you can't slip away unnoticed now – this clash is unavoidable.

Guard #1 (with Sword)	9⚡5🌿 ⊙5⇥⇤5🛡
Guard #2 (with Sword)	6⚡3🌿 ⊙6⇥⇤9🛡
Guard #3 (with Sword)	3⚡2🌿 ⊙7⇥⇤8🛡

If you win the battle, you can take **+4**✴ from the guards' pouches, hoping that this puts an end to the fighting (#208).

#23

The tunnel widens and opens into a comfortable little cavern where you no longer need to crawl hunched over. As you look around, there's not much to see, but you can head in several directions from here.

You can continue north (#239).

You can go west toward the narrow passage (#163).

You can head east (#282).

You can go south toward the darkness (#188).

#24

You're certain the others will return soon, so you don't have much time. You quickly search the tents, hoping to find something.

You find some ⦿ gold. Roll a die and multiply the result by 4, then add that amount of gold to your inventory.

You don't find much else of use in the camp; it's time to head back to the main road (#50).

#25

As you place the fish on the table, Knireek's eyes narrow, his lip curling in a snarl of offense. His hand instinctively drifts to the hilt of his dagger, knuckles whitening. "Do you take me for some stinking fisherman?" he growls, his voice low and simmering with indignation.

You hurriedly try to explain to him that it's fresh, caught this morning, delicious when cooked, but your words not landing well. The attempt only stokes the fire within him. Knireek leans forward, his face inches from yours, the tension palpable in the charged silence. "So now you'd have me slaving like a kitchen maid? A warrior reduced to gutting fish?" His glare is sharp enough to slice through steel, and the room feels suddenly too small, breathless with the weight of unspoken threats.

He slaps you for insulting him so rudely, and you tumble under the table, costing you **-1⚡** point in this little altercation, but at least you tried.

He says that since he likes your boldness, he'll give you a chance to put the fish away and come up with something more valuable for him.

If you have a 🧺**hooded cloak** and leave it as collateral (#323).

If you have a 🧺**leather glove** and leave it as collateral (#79).

If you have a 🧺**vial of elixir** and leave it as collateral (#226).

If you don't have any of these or simply don't trust them enough to leave anything behind, you can just stand up and walk back to the tavern counter (#195).

#26

You dash through a small street. The salty scent of the sea is carried toward you by the wind from somewhere.

The guards are hot on your heels.

You can go forward (#364), turn right toward the main road (#132), or turn left down a narrow street (#266).

#27

The fight in the middle of the night wakes the ship's crew, but by the time they rush to help, there's no one left to fight, so you just smile contentedly as they arrive. After the battle, you gain **+1** point and hope for a quiet night until dawn.

Indeed, no one disturbs you, and you manage to rest a bit, but the first rays of sunlight find you on the deck. Captain Rottora orders the anchor raised to continue the journey.

Soon, you arrive at **Ugmarlyther**, where you shake hands with the captain, thanking him for the trip and his help. Captain Rottora assures you that if you need a ship next time, you can always count on his.

You wave, hop off the deck, and head to check out the harbor (#96).

#28

You feel that, as painful as it is, it might be a good idea to leave the thorn in your foot for now.

If you decide to do so, note that you take a **-50** penalty in every battle until a healer helps you remove the thorn. It's a bearable inconvenience if you choose this path, and you can continue your adventure with the thorn in your foot from here (#218).

If you change your mind and decide to pull the thorn out of your foot right here (#103).

#29

You take out the jar of honey and offer it to him.

"Ah, honey!" he says, taking it from you and tasting it. "What do you want in return, my friend?"

You can ask for gold in exchange (#307).

You can ask about Kiena (#72).

You can ask who he is (#373).

You can ask about weapons (#334).

If you feel this situation is already creepy enough, you can head back through the forest to the main road (#50).

#30

You stride toward the gate, your footsteps echoing ominously. The guards' laughter dies abruptly, replaced by sharp, narrowed glares. As you approach, tension coils in the air like a taut wire. Two of them step forward abruptly, their hands resting on their weapons, blocking your path with rigid defiance.

"What's your business in 📖Dispel, stranger?!"

You have several options:

"I'm here to find Kiena. Where can I find her?" (#119)

"I just want to look around the city. I've heard a lot about the Citadel." (#249)

"I'd like to sell some fish." (#314)

Or you can casually wave them off, turn around, and try your luck at the marketplace (#181).

#31

You leave the bees and the farm behind, heading back along the well-trodden path toward the watchtower. The buzzing sounds quickly fade as you walk away (#289).

#32

You wander through the dense forest, spotting a few freshly cut trunks to your left.

You can go left from here (#352) or right (#367).

#33

This tunnel isn't much wider or more comfortable on the way back; you're still amazed you can even crawl forward in it. The lights grow dimmer behind you as you move away, and soon there's no question – you're crawling in complete darkness.

Breathing becomes harder in the damp, confined space. You thought the return trip would be easier, but you still have to stop to rest, as this short tunnel journey drains your energy, costing you **-2 ⚡** points.

At one point, the tunnel sharply turns almost back on itself and suddenly slopes downward. You slowly but surely slide down the damp, muddy chute, landing headfirst at the altar.

You shake yourself off, vowing not to go through that again unless absolutely necessary.

Still, you can examine the altar again (#371).

Or you can head toward the only exit, moving north along the corridor (#101).

#34

As you emerge from the cellar into the backyard, you hear the large gate opening from the outside, and it might be an easier escape through the gate than climbing back to the upper floor. You hide behind the opening gate, then see and hear someone, or more than one, bringing firewood into the yard. Fortunately, they head to the covered storage area at the far end. When both have their backs to the open gate, you carefully and unnoticed slip out.

From the back street, you easily find the way back to the main square.

You smile, relieved that you've successfully pulled off this little wine-stealing adventure (#348).

#35

You firmly shake your head.

"No, my friend," you say, reaching for the stone, "thirty gold, or no deal."

As you utter the words, one of Knireek's companions slowly rises, their piercing gaze locking onto yours. With a sudden, violent motion, they draw a knife and slam it into the table, the blade quivering ominously. The sharp crack of metal against wood echoes through the air despite the loud noise in the tavern, leaving no doubt — haggling with them would be a perilous mistake.

You're well aware that fighting is out of the question — they'd be too strong for you right now.

You can still accept the offered **20⊛** and walk out of the tavern (#143).

Or you can insist on demanding thirty gold for your efforts (#178).

#36

"Ah, yes, Kiena needs help, but Kiena trusts no one," he says, then retreats into his hut.

That was a pretty vague response.

You can try to coax him out again (#70), or if you think it's time to move on, you can leave this strange hut and its occupant behind and return to the main road (#50).

#37

You weave through a grim tapestry of white-gray corpses, their jagged forms glinting under a crimson-streaked sky. The air hums with an eerie stillness, broken only by your cautious steps. You search for something, anything, though its nature eludes you, a fleeting hope buried in the carnage. Suddenly, a sharp, dry clatter pierces the silence, like bones grinding against stone. Your pulse quickens. Around you, the fallen stir, their hollow sockets flaring with an unnatural emerald glow. Six skeleton warriors rise, their rusted blades gleaming with flecks of scarlet and violet light, closing in with menacing purpose.

Clearly, some kind of crimson-blue magic has brought them to life, perhaps a spell lingering over the battlefield.

Unfortunately, there's no real chance to flee now — it's time to draw your weapon and face whatever comes.

Skeleton #1 (with Sword)	17⚡4〽️ ⊙6→⊦←2🛡️
Skeleton #2 (with Sword)	21⚡5〽️ ⊙7→⊦←1🛡️
Skeleton #3 (with Sword)	19⚡3〽️ ⊙5→⊦←2🛡️
Skeleton #4 (with Sword)	20⚡5〽️ ⊙4→⊦←2🛡️
Skeleton #5 (with Sword)	19⚡5〽️ ⊙5→⊦←1🛡️
Skeleton #6 (with Sword)	14⚡4〽️ ⊙7→⊦←3🛡️

If you manage to defeat the skeletons, it might be time to reconsider whether it's worth lingering here a bit longer and perhaps checking the blue-crested corpses (#115), or if you feel leaving as quickly as possible (#269) that would be a good call as well.

#38

As Pap searches through the books, he explains that the books about the city's modern history are quite contradictory, while the writings from the era of the city's founders, even if penned by different hands, consistently describe events in the same way.

He tries to find you a reliable book containing the notes of the first settlers, written in a precise but difficult-to-understand ancient dialect.

While raising walls of stone here, fathers raised roofs over their families' heads, gates already receiving winding roofs, the likes of which this land had not seen before our arrival. Our torches are lit at night, their glow brighter than the stars' radiance that guided us across the rolling waters. Here it was, the divine Chole Gemoon Chemn, which we eat and drink, teaching our children to do the same, so that Dysp'l may prosper through the ages. Unbroken.

Their leader, the omnipotent Gaki Chakgrek, we obey and build for him. The woman who was strong enough to lead us here, this is written in the 33rd year of her life. Her moonbeam eyes and brown skin always command us, strength and roses guiding Gaki's steps. The raiser of the dead.

For her, the tower is built, and our spears protect her.

The tower and all that lies beneath it. Beneath our land, our treasures are buried, so our children may abound even in lean years, after Gaki. Gaki the mighty, the benevolent, the all-powerful.

From what you can gather from the text, the founders were enthusiastic builders who seem to hint at leaving treasures buried beneath the ground. Of course, it's possible these treasures — whatever they may be — have long since been found, or perhaps they're still there because they were deemed worthless, and no one ever bothered to look for them.

Are you interested in local legends? (#205)

Would you like to read about the Citadel? (#114)

Or have you had enough of legends and prefer to leave the bookstore for now? (#77)

#39

The road leads to a bridge, from where you can see the city gates in one direction, guarded by sentries as expected, while the other direction takes you toward the forest.

You can head toward the city gate (#20), choose the path leading to the forest (#130), or walk among the smaller houses outside the city gate (#356).

#40

With cautious steps, you approach the weathered wooden coffin resting atop a modest stone altar, its surface dusted with the faint shimmer of cobwebs catching the dim, flickering light of nearby candles. Your fingers tremble slightly as you grasp the splintered edge of the lid, lifting it with deliberate slowness, wary of any sudden surprises that might lurk within. As the lid creaks open, a faint musty scent wafts upward, and your eyes fall upon a single, breathtaking sight: an ornate sword, its blade gleaming with intricate engravings that dance like liquid silver under the soft glow. The hilt, adorned with vibrant gemstones — emeralds and sapphires that pulse with a quiet brilliance — seems almost out of place in this forgotten place. A wry smile tugs at your lips as the irony dawns: this tiny, desolate village, with its crumbling cottages and overgrown paths, appears so forsaken that not even the greediest of thieves would bother to plunder its treasures.

Just as you're about to reach for the sword, you hear a strange, dry rattling sound behind you. You quickly turn around and see two animated skeletons, appearing out of nowhere, brandishing swords and advancing toward you.

Skeleton #1 (with Sword)	9 ⚡ 0 🗡 ⊙4 →∦← 1 🛡
Skeleton #2 (with Sword)	9 ⚡ 1 🗡 ⊙5 →∦← 0 🛡

If you defeat the skeletons, your attention can turn back to the ornate sword in the coffin. Upon closer inspection, it's not just a sword with a gem-encrusted hilt but one adorned with red diamonds.

You take the sword in hand and immediately feel it wasn't forged for combat, only for decoration. The hilt digs into your palm, and the many colorful gems embedded in the hilt and parts of the blade completely throw off the weapon's balance.

Nevertheless, if you want to take it, you can add the 🗑️ →|← **red gem-encrusted sword (97-3)** to your inventory. It has ⊙3 →|← 2⬦-3 ◧ points.

You might never use it in combat, as its grip is quite uncomfortable (#329).

#41

The ascent to the Citadel is a breathtaking sight, a massive stone staircase adorned on both sides with purple and lemon-yellow flowers, all the way up to the top step. On each side, there are two statues — four in total — depicting large human figures, positioned symmetrically at the base and top of the staircase. You can't see clearly, but there seems to be a fifth statue at the top, in the center, depicting a female figure. The statues' pedestals bear inscriptions, likely about the figures they represent, but from this distance, you can't read them clearly. The years carved on them are slightly larger, but even those you can only guess at. You can't get any closer because the staircase leading to the Citadel is enclosed within another massive stone-walled garden, and the arched entrance is blocked by a huge iron gate, steadfastly guarded by two sentries.

The Citadel's servants clearly use some other route to move between the city and the inner garden, but you can't see where they come or go. There's likely a hidden gate in the walls. It seems unlikely that the main gate's bars have been raised recently.

If you have any business in the Citadel, you'll need to find another way to get there.

For now, there's little to do here except marvel at this structure, disproportionately grand for the size of the city — it's certainly impressive enough to be the pride of a capital.

Around you, people come and go, all moving with determined haste, making it unlikely you could ask anyone on the street for information.

You might try asking around in the tavern (#113), or if you prefer, you can lose yourself in the bustle, soaking in the city's vibrant energy (#229), or if you've had enough of the city center, you can head toward the gate (#149).

#42

You dash across the bridge and then try to slip away somewhere in the surrounding narrow streets.

The guards are hot on your heels.

You can go right (#15), forward (#246), or left (#342).

#43

You learn a great deal about that over time, the Citadel has been re-built several times, and drawings and illustrations from different eras show its periodic changes. Not only was it expanded externally, but its internal layout was also extensively modified for the more modern needs.

Several books mention that the Citadel originally consisted of a single tower on the hill, with additional wings added over time. One entry describes this in a very precise, engineering manner:

R aising the tower required foundational work underground to slow and ultimately halt its sinking. The underground extension became as large as the original tower itself. The plans were based on Chaklia Wi's vision, including the design of the (3-21) chambers and the connecting tunnels, which later became part of the sewer system.

A few pages later, another account discusses how the interior spaces were expanded and the central tower's area was enlarged:

T he original tower, due to its purpose, required expansion. Out of respect for Gaki's original intent, it must be renewed as the founders surely would have done as their numbers grew.

A second tower must be built beside the original, then the walls at their meeting point demolished and rebuilt at the outer arcs' intersection, all before the rainy season arrives.

The expansion was indeed impressive, and from the city gate, it's hard to tell exactly which parts of the Citadel were rebuilt just by looking at it.

The book also mentions that the roof structure of one wing burned down and had to be rebuilt:

In the 103rd year, a disastrous fire consumed both side wings entirely. Thanks to the residents' efforts, the fire was extinguished, but the city recognized the need for a sawmill.

Sufficient timber for the new roof had to be transported via the river.

The book also mentions a place called 📖**Ugmarlyther**, which, based on the descriptions, grew into a full-fledged city during this period due to its carpentry and logging industry.

These are fascinating details about the Citadel's structure, but it's unlikely you'll find much more useful information in the books.

If you'd like, you can read more about the Citadel on another topic (#114), or you can leave the books behind and continue your adventure in the fresh air (#77).

#44

You tell Jarse that you'd love to help, but Freela didn't mention that it would cost anything, and you don't have enough gold on you.

You promise to gather the gold and return later.

Feeling awkward, you step out of the hut, but Jarse's friendly demeanor leaves no doubt that you're welcome back anytime.

From the path in front of the hut, you can head in two directions: north toward the bridge (#39), or east, following the city wall among the houses (#238).

#45

You walk back to the corridor, and as you leave the room with the coffin, the stone door closes behind you with a deep rumble (#191).

#46

You stand at the bottom of the stairs, where stray beams of light filter in from here and there, allowing you to roughly make out where the tunnel continues.

You can go north through the narrow tunnel (#188).

Or you can climb up the stairs (#391).

#47

"Ah, Kiena needs help. Many want the stones, and she's not strong enough to face them alone," he says, then retreats into his hut.

That was a pretty vague response.

You can try to coax him out again (#70), or if you think it's time to move on, you can leave this strange hut and its occupant behind and return to the main road (#50).

#48

The corridor indeed ends in a large chamber, which likely once served as a prayer room, judging by the altar on the wall and the now half-rotted and decayed wooden pews. Most of these pews have been tossed against the wall, suggesting someone needed space to easily remove a valuable object, perhaps even a complete part of the altar.

You can examine the rotten pews if you're interested (#146).

You can take a closer look at the altar — or what's left of it (#311).

There's only one exit from this chamber, leading back through the corridor you came from (#101).

#49

At the harbor, you spot familiar faces. Captain Devismore and his crew are still sorting and packing their bountiful catch into crates, likely to take to the fish market soon. He gives you a friendly wave when he sees you, which you return kindly.

Beneath a bruised sky, a cluster of weathered ships sways at the dock, their creaking hulls poised to flee with tomorrow's ghostly dawn tide. You weave through the salty throng, desperation clinging to your inquiries about destinations, passage, and cost. The answers are bleak — most captains, their eyes glinting with the cold sheen of gold coins, scoff at the notion of passengers, naming prices so exorbitant they seem to mock your plight. A few ships might carry you, but their courses veer toward uncharted realms or back to the shores you've already fled, leaving hope to find Kiena as dim as the fading horizon.

After some quick inquiries, one ship catches your interest: Captain Rottora is sailing up the 🗺**Shorough River** all the way to 🗺**Ugmarlyther**.

You can talk to Captain Devismore (#283).

You can talk to Captain Rottora (#207).

You can leave the harbor toward the fish market (#320) or head to the city marketplace (#181).

#50

Following your own tracks back, you navigate the dense forest with ease. Soon, you notice the trees thinning out, and more sunlight filters through the branches (#130).

#51

You step out of the watchtower through the thick oak door and find yourself back at the main street's junction. Looking north, you can clearly see the source of the smoke column — a small house in the middle of a fenced farm. Next to and around the house are various-sized wooden boxes standing on legs.

You can return to the watchtower if you wish (#329).

Or you can head along the main street toward the tavern (#199).

You can also set off toward the farm (#222).

#52

The door opens with a loud creak, leaving you no time to closely inspect what lies beyond (#13).

#53

You're running down a small side street somewhere in the city center.

The guards are hot on your heels.

You can go right (#315) or left toward the main street (#372).

#54

You spend some time here, feeling along the wall for any known opening mechanisms, but the barred segment of the wall seems to have grown out of the tunnel wall itself, leaving no clues how to open it.

There are no recesses or hidden levers on either side of the walls around the grate that might open it. Regardless, it's clear that if you want to reach the cross-tunnel on the other side of the wall, it can only be done from another direction.

It's time to head back through the tunnel and choose another path (#23).

#55

The narrow path you're traveling on doesn't seem to be used often. Weeds have overgrown its edges, and in some places, bushes and branches lean over the path so much that you almost have to force your way through. The rustling of leaves from one bush and the faint noises coming from behind it make you instinctively pause and reach for your weapon.

If this is your first time here (#211), or if you've been on this path before (#148).

#56

You stand in a chamber where a ladder leads upward, through which the locals are diligently passing up buckets filled with mud.

On the right side of the circular chamber, there's a small grated opening through which you can see another room with an altar, also completely submerged in water and mud.

From here, you can try to climb up the ladder (#144) or move forward through a smaller, mud-covered corridor leading out of the chamber (#353).

#57

You tell the bartender that you're looking for a friend, Kiena, who likely passed through here a few days ago, and you're curious about where she might have gone next.

The bartender says someone by that name was here, but she was very quiet, didn't talk to anyone, and left quickly. He could not even recall the person's face, he only remembers her because she wore a long black hood, and such mysterious figures don't often come around.

This is a quiet little town, not on the usual route for travelers, who mostly head south toward Dig and 📖**Whitpoint** after they landed on the shore. It strikes you as odd that Kiena would come here, and you ask the bartender about it, but he doesn't know much more. Maybe she arrived by boat on the river or came to meet someone in town, but if so, it's a mystery to him.

You can ask about the event in the main square (#259).

Or you can dive into the bustle of the main square if you feel there's nothing more for you here (#107).

#58

The workshop is empty; Ifer must have gone somewhere, perhaps back to the forest to check on his apprentice. You look around but find nothing interesting aside from the massive log, now sawed in half on the workbench.

For now, you simply walk back out to the street (#77).

#59

"Hold it, stranger!" one of the guards shouts, pointing his spear at you.

"I just want to enter the city."

"Outsiders stay outside!" he says in a tone that brooks no argument.

You realize you won't get through the gate without force, and violence isn't the best choice right now. It's better to head somewhere else.

In the direction of the river, you see the signs of a few small workshops (#77).

The clamor of the marketplace (#181) can be heard from here.

#60

This isn't the most upscale area; the city's poorest live here along the riverbank, just beneath the city wall, in small and large huts and tents.

You spot a grated sewer opening between two tents by the roadside.

> If you have 🔑 **a rusty key**, you can use it here by writing its numbers side by side, adding them to this chapter's number, and continuing at the resulting chapter.
>
> If you have 💡 **a map** that marks secret passages, you can use it here by multiplying the two numbers on the map, adding the result to this chapter's number, and continuing at the resulting chapter.

A straight path leads from here to the riverbank, taking you back to the harbor (#1).

Or, heading up the street, you can revisit the small artisan workshops (#77).

#61

If this is the first time you want to examine the maps (#124), or if you've already done so before (#235).

#62

You stand next to the huge barrels, where a small rack holds bottles of wine already filled, waiting to be served. From above, you hear the muffled hum of the tavern, but for now, no one seems to be coming down here.

You can easily take 🧺**a bottle of this local wine (17-5)**, which you can drink at any time for a one-time gain of **+6⚡** points.

If you have a 🧺**flask filled with water**, you can refill it with this fine wine. If you do, note that this wine will grant **+6⚡** points when you decide to drink it.

As tempting as it may be, you can't go straight up the stairs to the tavern from here, so you have no choice but to climb back to the room you came from (#34).

#63

You step out of the mill and head back toward the marketplace along the winding dirt path through the wheat fields. It doesn't take long to walk down the hill and reach the first houses. The clamor of the marketplace grows louder, and soon you find yourself in the midst of the bustle (#6).

#64

The door swings open with a whisper, revealing the grandeur of the entrance hall beyond. You step into a breathtaking foyer, where opulent red velvet curtains cascade down the walls like streams of crimson wine, their rich hue glowing warmly in the soft flicker of crystal chandeliers overhead. The air hums with an almost tangible sense of extravagance. Adorning the walls, vibrant paintings burst with color — sweeping landscapes of emerald valleys and sapphire skies, alongside portraits of enigmatic figures whose eyes seem to follow your every move with quiet intensity. Each gilded frame and polished artifact gleams with undeniable value, whispering of treasures ripe for the taking in this lavish domain. At the heart of the hall, a grand staircase spirals upward, its polished mahogany steps and intricate golden balustrades beckoning you toward the mysteries that await above.

You hear noises and voices from upstairs — you're not alone in the house!

Roll two dice. If the result is higher than your 🌀 points, you unfortunately failed to stay silent and unnoticed; continue the story at #13.

Luckily, you haven't made any noise so far. Two doors lead from here: you can go through the right-hand door (#192) or the left-hand door (#278).

If you feel it's time to leave the house, you can do so (#145).

#65

The fountain is a fine piece of craftsmanship, particularly in terms of its stonework. It likely once consisted of two parts: a lower basin and an upper section fixed to the center of the basin, possibly carved from a solid block. It's impossible to say for sure, but a statue or some other carving probably stood here. Over the years, someone must have taken it, likely because it might have been adorned with valuable gems, making it worth breaking off its base and hauling through the tunnel. The lower part of the fountain would probably have been stolen too, but as far as you can tell, its foundation extends deep into the ground, as you can't even make it budge.

The outer edge of the basin was likely decorated with gems in its peak, but you see that all of them have already been taken, leaving only the empty settings behind. In some places, even those are gone, likely pried out with a heavy tool like a hammer or axe in the quickest and easiest way possible.

You don't find anything else useful from examining the fountain.

You can try clearing the debris from the north-leading corridor (#8).

Or you can head south, past the broken iron bars, crawling through the increasingly narrow tunnel (#163).

#66

The old man invites you in and tells you he's the healer in town, his name is Mog B'son. Luckily, he has some remedies and ointments in his satchel, and judging by your appearance, he agrees you could use some care.

He sizes you up and says that for a small fee, he can take good care of you.

If you want to and can pay him **10**⊛ (#189), or if you think that's too much for his services and decide to move on (#322).

#67

The roasting spit stands empty above the now faintly smoldering hearth.

The air carries a gentle warmth as you settle onto the soft, sun-dappled grass, the faint hum of contentment surrounding you. Long ago, the village dogs gleefully gobbled up the scraps of meat that tumbled to the ground, but that small mishap has done nothing to dim the radiant joy of the gathering. A sturdy new table stands proudly nearby, adorned with a colorful spread of golden-crusted bread, creamy wedges of cheese, and vibrant fruits — plump grapes and rosy apples glistening in the soft afternoon light. The villagers' laughter weaves through the air like a soothing melody, their voices rising and falling as they toast to the bountiful harvest to come.

A little farther off, the dogs now frolic in playful chase, their carefree bounds stirring gentle ripples in the tall meadow grass, kissed by the golden glow of the setting sun. You tear off a warm, crusty piece of bread, its comforting aroma wrapping around you like a soft blanket. As you nibble, leaning back against the earth, you watch the villagers' tireless celebration — their faces aglow with warmth and unity, swaying to the faint strum of a distant lute. Though you know you won't linger until the festivities fade into the starlit night, this tranquil moment of rest feels like a gentle embrace, refreshing your spirit and filling your heart with quiet peace.

After swallowing the last bite, you slowly stand up, brush the grass off your clothes, and head back through the houses toward the marketplace.

After a short walk, you're already there (#6).

#68

You keep running down a small street, with the city wall looming to your right.

The guards are hot on your heels.

You can go right (#346) or keep running forward (#305).

#69

You linger in front of the tavern for a while, but nothing interesting catches your eye. People come and go, and one of them drops a purse. Your eyes light up briefly, but when you see the old man notice and turn back for it, the smile fades from your face.

No luck this time.

You can head toward the Citadel (#41), or leave the city through the Wamake gate (#149).

If you've had enough of the fresh air, you can go back into the tavern (#113).

#70

You approach the hut, and there seems to be no movement around it.

Just a few steps from the entrance, the door swings open, and a hooded figure emerges from the dim interior. Their face is completely hidden in the shadows, making it impossible to discern who they are.

"Ah, have you finally brought the honey?" they ask in a friendly tone, extending their arm toward you.

You're so surprised by the question that you don't move for a moment, but they continue.

"Or perhaps the wine?" they ask again.

You remain frozen by the unexpected directness.

If you have a 🧺 **jar of honey** and want to give it to them (#29).

If you have a 🧺 **flask filled with wine** and want to give it to them (#262).

If you'd rather draw your weapon (#379).

If you feel this is a rather bizarre situation and would prefer to leave it behind, you can cautiously back away and return to the main road (#50).

#71

You slowly start to move away from the altar, and after a few steps, the gloomy blue light completely fades.

You feel that you've left a worthy offering on the altar for the God of Abundance (#224).

#72

"Oh, Kiena, a beautiful creature. She's after the stones. Why are you looking for her?"

You can reply that you're also searching for the stones and Kiena could help you (#366).

Or you can say that Kiena is your friend and you want to help her (#36).

#73

This little encounter with the wildlife caused a few tense moments, but it doesn't deter you from continuing your journey.

You can head west – slightly northwest (#343).

Or you can go east – slightly southeast (#240).

#74

Using the map, you effortlessly locate the grated opening, and indeed, the bars haven't been repaired — they swing open with the slightest push, revealing a narrow, dark tunnel. You crawl through the seemingly endless passage, which is barely more than ten yards long. A few rats scurry past in the opposite direction, paying you no mind, chattering in their high-pitched squeaks.

The other end of the tunnel is open, and following the filtering light, you quickly find yourself on the other side of the wall. Fortunately, no one is around when you emerge from the sewer opening, so you simply blend into the not-too-crowded city center bustle.

Looking to your right, you see the stairs leading up to the Citadel, though the gated entrance blocks the way. You can try your luck there (#41), or visit the tavern in the central square — someone there might have heard of Kiena and could help you find her (#113). If you'd rather just wander in the city's hustle for now, you can do that first (#229).

Alternatively, you can walk out through the main gate and leave the inner city (#149).

#75

You approach the small campsite of seven, maybe eight tents, cleverly hidden among the dense trees and bushes, with determined steps. As you get closer, two bandits guarding the camp immediately charge at you, snarling.

This is going to be a fight to the death.

Bandit #1 (with Sword)	10⚔6↻ ⦿5→|←7🛡
Bandit #2 (with Sword)	14⚔6↻ ⦿7→|←6🛡

If, by some miracle, you survive the battle (#24).

#76

He's not surprised when you ask about Kiena, as if he's been waiting to talk about her. He tells you she stayed here about two days ago, looking to find a wizard in the southern forests. He's heard rumors of a demon wizard setting up camp in the dense forest, but no one he knows has ever met them.

Supposedly, it's quite hard to find the wizard because they constantly move their hut's location — though he adds again that this is just hearsay. He doesn't believe it, as the wizard would have no reason to hide. Still, if they truly live in the forest, they must lead a very quiet, hermit-like life.

All he knows is that Kiena was searching for this wizard and asked for directions to 🗺**Whitpoint**, where she planned to continue by ship. Oreth tries to recall the name of the ship Kiena inquired about, and after some thought, he remembers it was called something like Faded Dogs or Burnt Dogs. If he recalls correctly, she's heading across the Neaera Sea toward the abandoned fortress of Hery Runes. He doesn't know what her business would be there, but according to him, she seemed in a hurry, staying only one night and generously paying for her lodging and food, which is why he remembers her clearly.

He adds that this isn't particularly noteworthy; many travelers pass through here and leave quickly, as this is the shortest route between 🗺**Dispel** and 🗺**Whitpoint**.

You thank him for the information, Oreth has shared genuinely useful details, and for free, however he did not seem convincing enough at every details, but some of the places he mentioned you have already heard of.

You can ask him about the local wine (#357).

You can sit at an empty table and order food or drink (#109).

You can inquire about the reasons for the increased guard presence (#200).

You can ask for a room to rest temporarily (#18).

You can look around the tavern and check out the people drinking there (#395).

Or you can leave the tavern and head back to the main square (#348).

#77

Along the river, there are a few small artisan shops. From their signs, you can tell that one is likely a carpenter's workshop (#155), another sells small hand tools (#217), and the third appears to be a small bookstore (#139).

The street continues further, and as far as you can see, it's mostly lined with residential houses and huts, but you never know what you might find in that direction (#60).

#78

You wander through the dense forest, spotting a few freshly cut trunks to your right.

You can go left (#384), forward (#352), or right (#286).

#79

You pull out the comfortable leather glove you took from Ifer and place it on the table as collateral. Knireek examines it for a while, asking if the glove has any magical properties. You shake your head, saying you know of no such powers, wisely keeping quiet about the fact that it came from a shabby carpenter's workshop.

Knireek shoves the glove back at you with a dismissive sneer, his eyes glinting with disdain as he declares it utterly unworthy of his finely crafted armor. "This won't do," he snaps, voice dripping with scorn. "If you've got anything better, you'd best dig it up — now."

Just as you start to tuck the glove away, one of Knireek's companions leans forward, eyes sparkling with excitement, and exclaims, "Wait, I love that glove!" Knireek shoots a quick glance at his companion, a flicker of curiosity in his gaze, before snatching the glove from your hand with a swift, eager motion. He tosses it to his companion, who catches it with a delighted grin, swiftly slipping the glove onto his hand. The leather gleams as he flexes his fingers, his face lighting up with pure satisfaction, as if the glove was crafted just for him.

It seems you'll have to part with the leather glove — at least for now, until you get it back — but since the group accepted your collateral, it's time to talk seriously about the details. They look at you, expecting you to share what you know about the Citadel's construction.

> If you know 💡**the unique structure of the Citadel's chamber system**, you can share it with them by writing the three digits of the chamber system side by side, subtracting this chapter's number from it, and continuing at the resulting chapter.

If you want to offer them something else, you can do so at any time.

If you have a 🧺**large basket of fish** and leave it as collateral (#25).

If you have a 🧺**hooded cloak** and leave it as collateral (#323).

If you have a 🧺**vial of elixir** and leave it as collateral (#226).

If you don't have any of these or simply don't trust them enough to leave anything behind, you can stand up and walk back to the tavern counter (#195).

#80

"Oh, Kiena, a clever creature. She's after the stones. Why are you looking for her?"

You can reply that you're also searching for the stones and Kiena could help you (#375).

Or you can say that Kiena is your friend and you want to help her (#47).

#81

You step closer to the fountain, and suddenly, two skeletons emerge from either side of it, advancing toward you. You have just enough time to quickly draw your weapons and try to be a worthy opponent.

Skeleton #1 (with Sword)	18 ⚡ 5 🗡 ⊙7 →⊩← 8 🛡
Skeleton #2 (with Sword)	17 ⚡ 6 🗡 ⊙6 →⊩← 7 🛡

If you successfully survive this little surprise, you'll see that there's nothing in the room beyond the fountain. However, the pleasant sound of trickling water relaxes you and somehow lifts your spirits, so deep in the dungeons, add **+3 🗡** and **+5 ⚡** points to yourself.

The narrow corridor leading north is the only way out. You crawl back through the opening, which eventually leads you back to the junction you came from not long ago (#277).

#82

A chill hangs in the air as you lean closer, your voice low and urgent, asking if Kiena has passed through these parts in your desperate search for her. Kokary's eyes, glinting with a cold, calculating smile, rake over you, sizing you up like a predator assessing its prey. He leans back, the faint creak of his chair slicing through the tense silence of the tavern. With a subtle, almost mocking tilt of his head, he murmurs, his voice smooth but edged with ice, "In my establishment, friend, information like that carries a price."

You can give him **1**⊛ to see if that loosens his tongue (#272).

Or you can ask him about the unusually high bustle in the village (#268).

Alternatively, you can leave and head back to the marketplace (#6).

#83

You sprint through a small street, with the river's outline visible to your right.

The guards are hot on your heels.

You can go left, back toward the main street (#377), or right (#383).

#84

You travel along a narrow dirt path lined with bushes and trees. To the east, you see the bushes and trees growing denser, leading into a forest.

The path continues east (#158) or northwest (#12).

#85

You kneel beside the wooden chest and see that its lid is not sealed. You carefully try to open it, but time has not been kind — the chest is completely rotted, a miracle it's still intact. The lid doesn't open when you touch it; instead, it crumbles into dust and breaks into smaller pieces under your hands.

Inside the chest, there were once papyrus scrolls, but as you touch them, they feel like sand, turning to dust beneath your fingers in an instant. Whatever was in this chest, and whatever those scrolls might have contained, it's now irretrievably lost to decay. No one will ever know their contents.

There's a single small gold coin in the chest; if you want, you can take this **1**⊛ with you.

The pile of hay in the other corner might still be inviting (#339).

Or, failing that, you can walk out of the cell (#280).

#86

He's crafting spears for the local guard, as there have been several raids in the area recently, and they're trying to catch the thieves. He doesn't know how many they've caught so far, but he does know that those they apprehend face the gallows. He's heard rumors that some of the thieves might be hiding in the southern forests, but no one has found their hideout yet — the forest is too dense, and a demon wizard supposedly resides there, discouraging even the most determined bounty hunters.

He then tells you he prefers making bows and arrows, having become quite a master at crafting these weapons. If you're curious, he'd be happy to show you his latest piece, which its buyer has yet to claim despite paying for it weeks ago. Something might have happened to the poor soul.

If you haven't seen his masterpiece and are curious, you can take a look (#390).

If you haven't already, you can ask about Kiena (#298).

Or you can bid him a friendly farewell and head north along the road (#156) or west, following the city wall (#356).

#87

You stand in a room with a floor covered in the same ornate stones you saw on your way here. In one corner, there's an empty stone altar, perhaps a raised bed or even a tomb. In the opposite corner, you see a small, lonely chest.

On one wall, there's a grated gate, and on another, a small opening leading to a corridor.

You can examine the small chest (#309).

You can try to open the grated gate (#245).

You can start exploring the corridor (#152).

Or you can crawl back through the narrow, damp tunnel you came from (#33).

#88

The essential oil works its magic, and you walk briskly past the dazed guards toward the city's central square. By the time they come to, you'll already be deep in the city's bustle.

The town's main square, contrary to what the massive city walls might suggest, is surprisingly small despite the imposing fortifications (#348).

#89

You slowly crawl through the tunnel, perhaps halfway through, when you spot a recess in the sidewall.

If this is your first time here (#167), or if you've been here before (#316).

#90

Next to the flower vase, you spot the sought-after 🧺**golden statue (13-4)**, which is quite peculiar: it depicts a stout, bald man sitting on the ground with his legs tucked under and hands clasped. It's an unusual sight, but you came to take the statue, not to admire it.

As you carefully reach for it, but you misjudge its weight — this statue must truly be solid gold. As you lift it, you lose your balance, knocking over the flower vase, which falls with a loud crash, rolls off the table, and shatters into pieces (#13).

#91

You slowly reach another junction. More precisely, the road leads to a bridge by a small river. Crossing the bridge, the road continues steadfastly south, but the signpost only points to Dig, which is far beyond the empire's borders — too far to travel on foot.

> If you've heard of 💡**the Battle of T'lindilhei**, you can head toward the battlefield by multiplying the two numbers, adding the result to this chapter's number, and continuing the story there.

To the west, however, a narrower path branching off the stone road leads to the port city of 📖**Whitpoint**, within reachable distance (#159).

Or you can head north along the wide stone road, which, according to the signpost, leads to 📖**Dispel** (#225).

#92

You wander through the dense forest, spotting white flowers to your left and a few freshly cut trunks to your right.

You can go left (#338) or right (#134).

#93

With a warm grin, you brush off Ifer's offer of payment, insisting that helping a friend is reward enough. Ifer's weathered face softens with surprise, and he hands you a worn leather glove, its soft texture promising a better grip. Together, you face the massive, dew-slicked log, its rough bark glistening under the morning sun. You both strain to hoist it onto the saw-bench, but the log's wet surface and scarce handholds make it a stubborn foe, slipping under your fingers with every heave.

During one attempt, the log lurches free, pulling you off balance. You instinctively reach for it, but its weight drags you down, and you hit the ground hard, bruising your arm for **-1⚡** point. Undaunted, you and Ifer rally, muscles burning as you finally roll the log onto the bench with a triumphant thud. Ifer sets to work, the pedal saw's rhythmic creak slicing through the wood, sending curls of sawdust into the air as the log yields into neat pieces, your shared effort glowing with quiet pride.

It seems Ifer is managing perfectly now, and since you didn't expect payment, you watch him work for a moment, a bit unsure. Either way, you've done what you could, and it's time to leave the carpenter's workshop (#176).

#94

You step back and charge to push the door open with as much force as possible.

The door doesn't budge, and you bounce off the sturdy structure like a ball. You feel your shoulder strain — this attempt costs you **-3⚡** points.

Of course, if you have a sword, you can try to pry the door open with it (#325).

Or you can walk back to the spiral staircase you came from (#263).

#95

You mention Kiena's name and ask if they've heard of her. They glance at each other for a moment, then shrug, saying they've never heard the name in their lives before resuming their laughing and drinking.

If you have **6**✳, you can buy the group a bottle of wine and try to pry some information out of them (#349).

Or you can leave them and talk to the bartender instead (#281).

#96

You stand in the harbor, where the bustle is immense. Several ships have just arrived, and with great enthusiasm and noise, their cargo is being unloaded onto small carts, which are eagerly pushed up a street to the northeast, likely toward the marketplace. Not far from here, a small bridge arches over the river.

You have no intention of helping with the unloading, so you can choose from three directions: northeast, where the carts are being pushed (#107), southeast along the narrow street by the riverbank (#276), or southwest, crossing the bridge (#169).

#97

You mention Kiena's name, and you can tell it strikes a chord with Freela. He knows exactly who you're talking about. He eyes you suspiciously and asks what your business is with Kiena.

You explain that you're searching for the lost stones and are certain that, even if Kiena doesn't know the exact location of all the stones, she knows where one is, and you want to ask her about it. Beyond that, you have no other business with her.

He asks what you'll do if Kiena doesn't reveal the stone's hiding place. You reply that you won't give up the search but need to try talking to her to find out. You share that you come from the northern continent and reveal your purpose for seeking the stones. It's not really Freela's business, but you figure it can't hurt to be open, as your intentions are honest.

Freela nods understandingly and tells you that Kiena was looking for a wizard named Nold Syanke in the area. He can't say exactly where the wizard's hideout is, but legend places it somewhere deep in the northern forests.

He also mentions that the wizard loves fine wines, so if you plan to visit him at his hideout, you should definitely bring some wine — it could do you a lot of good. He adds that Kiena was here at the tavern about two days ago, searching for Nold Syanke. She was a quiet traveler, stayed one night, and then moved on. Freela didn't talk much with her; she was quite reserved and only asked about the wizard. Perhaps you could get something out of the wizard if you find his hideout in the forest.

Freela slaps your table, saying it's time to order another pint. If you have 2⚙, you can order another (#150).

If you think you're done here at the tavern, you can walk out (#394).

#98

You stop in front of the outdoor tables where various tools, both small and large, are displayed for sale. You can't even guess the purpose of most of them. The workshop's owner, an elderly woman, approaches you and gruffly barks that her name is Azdunn, everything on the table is for sale, but she won't buy any junk from you.

Without waiting for your response, she immediately steps away and starts talking to another interested customer.

You can take a closer look at the items on offer (#397), or you can leave Azdunn and move on (#77).

#99

You briskly step onto the dirt path leading toward 📖**Oceastall**, quickening your pace as the beautifully sparkling sunlight warms your skin.

As you approach the village, you see more and more golden wheat fields swaying in the breeze, and by the time you reach the first houses, they nearly fill the horizon. A single structure towers above the houses nearby – a large windmill, its sails slowly turned by the gentle wind.

The village has one main street, winding between small huts and leading straight to the village center, the marketplace (#6).

#100

As you step closer to the altar, it begins to glow more intensely with an otherworldly blue gloomy light. The closer you try to get, the stronger this mysterious blue light pushes you back, keeping you at a distance from the altar. You try reaching out with just your hand, but it feels like hitting a solid wall at a certain point.

You attempt the same with your sword, but the sensation is identical — as if an invisible barrier stands between you and the altar. It's now clear why no one has touched the altar; it doesn't allow anyone to approach.

You have no idea how to get closer to it, so you can either leave the chamber to the west, where you see another room submerged in water (#186), or head southeast into a completely empty chamber (#17).

#101

You walk comfortably along this corridor adorned with ornate stones. About halfway through, you notice a grated recess on one side. You examine the grate but find no lock or hinge on the structure.

In the dim light, you see no recesses or levers on the walls on either side that might open the grate. You tug at it slightly, but it remains firmly in place. It's clear that the small, dark tunnel beyond the grate can only be accessed from somewhere else.

You can head north, where this wide tunnel seems to end (#142).

Or you can go south, where the outlines of a much larger chamber begin to take shape (#48).

#102

You quickly climb down the ladder while the locals take a short break (#56).

#103

Pulling the thorn out of your foot will undoubtedly be painful.

> If you do pull out the thorn, it will immediately cost you **-6⚡** points. If you have enough ⚡ points to remain alive afterward, you can continue your adventure from here (#218).

If you change your mind and decide to bandage the wound instead, planning to seek proper medical help later (#28).

#104

You place a gleaming **3⊛** on the table.

"For the sake of an old friendship, let's settle on this," you say with a smile, and he pockets your gold without batting an eye (#230).

#105

As you move through the narrow tunnel, you feel it gently curving until it opens into a small, chamber-like hollow. This small room must have once been sealed off from the rest of the tunnel, but now all you see is a rusted iron grate, broken away from the wall, that once blocked this direction.

You walk past the grate, and in the center of the room, you spot a fountain that hasn't worked in ages, judging by the debris and dust filling it, with weeds growing around it in places.

To the north, there was once an exit tunnel, but it's now hopelessly collapsed, with massive stone rubble blocking what was once a passageway.

You can try clearing the debris from the north-leading corridor (#8).

You can examine the fountain more closely (#65).

Or you can head south, past the broken iron bars, crawling through the increasingly narrow tunnel (#163).

#106

You travel along a narrow dirt path lined with bushes and trees. To the west, it seems the trees and bushes grow denser, leading through a forested area.

The path continues west (#297) or east (#12).

#107

You stand in the bustling heart of the marketplace, where countless vendors are trying to sell their wares. On a platform, you spot a small, noisy group — whether they're performers or merchants, you're not sure, but their loud voices are certainly drawing curious onlookers.

Across the square, the tavern stands, not seeming particularly crowded at the moment.

If you want to take a closer look at the noisy group on the platform (#302).

You can pop into the tavern if you haven't been there yet (#216).

You can head southwest toward the harbor (#96), or leave the square by following a narrower street northeast (#387).

#108

The debris conceals a flask, likely left behind by a previous visitor to this dungeon and later covered by falling dust and small rubble.

You unscrew the flask's cap and cautiously sniff it, detecting no distinct smell — it seems like water. You'd give anything for a mug of strong wine to ease the pain in your foot.

Nevertheless, the 🗑flask filled with water could still come in handy if you want to take it with you.

There's nothing else interesting to see here, and you hope you won't trigger any more hidden traps.

You can head north back into the tunnel (#234).

Or you can pass through the arched opening to another very similar chamber to the northwest (#183).

#109

You sit down at an empty table in a secluded corner, and the tavern keeper soon comes over to ask what you'd like to eat or drink.

You can order a cup of local wine for **2**⊛, which grants you **+1**⚡ point, or a slice of freshly roasted meat for **3**⊛, which gives you **+2**⚡ points if you pay for it.

You can also ask the tavern keeper about anything (#281).

You can look around to see who's sitting nearby, hoping to find interesting company (#395).

Or, if you've seen enough, you can leave the tavern (#348).

#110

After the fight, you gain **+1**🐇 point and can peacefully return to dine on the tender young rabbit, which has roasted to perfection and grants you **+4**⚡ points before you sleep.

After dinner, you toss a few larger pieces of wood onto the fire, then curl up under your cloak, close to the warmth, and drift off to sleep. The fire slowly dies out beside you, leaving only a smoldering pile of weak embers by dawn.

In the morning, you gather yourself and continue your journey toward 🗺 **Moonward** (#12).

#111

The altar is utterly captivating, a masterpiece of fine craftsmanship — or at least it was until someone decided to smash it. Whether out of anger or in search of something, you'll never know.

It's not entirely clear which notable religious event the ornate motifs depict, as they include many small illustrations you've never seen or even encountered of. That's not surprising, given your limited knowledge of the Duland Heirs' religion, aside from a few fragmented stories. But it's also possible that this dates back to an earlier era, the work of an entirely different congregation, left behind in the tunnels during renovations and rebuilds, at the mercy of adventurous fortune-seekers.

You become completely engrossed as you touch and run your fingers over the finely polished curves. Suddenly, one of the larger pieces falls out from the rest — ironically, as if only prayer had been holding it in place all this time.

A pang of unease hits you, fearing that the altar's remaining beauty is crumbling because of you, but your concern quickly turns to curiosity when you glimpse a tunnel behind it. Your worry vanishes in an instant, and using the leg of one of the pews, you pry off more pieces of the altar to fully expose the tunnel's entrance.

Your hard demolition work pays off, and the tunnel entrance is now completely clear.

If you wish, you can crawl into the tunnel behind the altar right now (#160).

If you're not ready to crawl again, you can examine the rotten pews (#146).

Or you can leave the prayer chamber for now, heading through the northern corridor (#101).

#112

You head toward the table.

If this is your first time examining the table (#172), or if you've been here before (#251).

#113

You step through the tavern door, greeted by a lively clamor. The restrictions on outsiders entering the city don't seem to dampen the atmosphere – plenty of people are drinking and laughing boisterously. Every table is occupied, with some patrons slumped over, fast asleep from too much drink.

The festive crowd barely notices you, singing and toasting with grand gestures as if celebrating something. Drinks splash everywhere, and a cheerful mood fills the air.

If you know 💡**which table is waiting for you**, you can sit there by multiplying the two numbers under the antlers decorating the pillar, adding the result to this chapter's number, and continuing at the resulting chapter.

You can also head to the counter to order something (#195).

You can sit next to one of the sleeping patrons (#212).

You can join a lone drinker at their table (#337).

Or you can leave the tavern and return to the city (#143).

#114

The Citadel is one of 📖**Dispel's** crown jewels, and countless books cover it. Pap asks what specifically interests you about the Citadel, offering to find some useful books on the topic.

Its structural design? (#43)

The original founders' goals? (#301)

The ancestors who owned it? (#253)

Or would you rather read about 📖**Dispel's** history instead? (#38)

Perhaps the surrounding legends pique your interest? (#205)

Or you can leave the bookstore and seek adventures outside (#77).

#115

You cautiously wander among the blue-crested corpses, searching for something — anything — though you're not sure what until you spot it. As you carefully avoid touching anything, you hear strange, dry rattling sounds. Around you, several corpses begin to stir, and within moments, you see about six skeleton warriors approaching you.

Clearly, some kind of crimson-whitish magic has brought them to life, perhaps a spell lingering over the battlefield.

Unfortunately, there's no real chance to flee now — it's time to draw your weapon and face whatever comes.

Skeleton #1 (with Sword)	16 ⚡5 ⟳ ⊙7 →∣← 2 🛡
Skeleton #2 (with Sword)	17 ⚡6 ⟳ ⊙6 →∣← 1 🛡
Skeleton #3 (with Sword)	21 ⚡4 ⟳ ⊙6 →∣← 3 🛡
Skeleton #4 (with Sword)	18 ⚡5 ⟳ ⊙4 →∣← 2 🛡
Skeleton #5 (with Sword)	13 ⚡5 ⟳ ⊙3 →∣← 1 🛡
Skeleton #6 (with Sword)	14 ⚡3 ⟳ ⊙7 →∣← 2 🛡

If you manage to defeat the skeletons, it might be time to reconsider whether it's worth lingering here and perhaps checking the blue-crested corpses (#37), or if you should leave as quickly as possible (#296).

#116

This desolate village sends chills down your spine; it's probably best to leave it behind.

You head back along the same road you took to reach the village. The abandoned, worn path winds slowly through the gentle hills, and after a while, you can no longer see the village when you look back (#55).

#117

"This is a boring town; nothing noteworthy happens here since they stopped letting outsiders into the city". He pauses for a moment and looks at you, as if wondering how you got in, but then says nothing more, just listlessly wipes the spilled drinks off the tavern counter.

You can sit at one of the quiet tables where someone is already slumped over, fast asleep (#212).

Or you can join someone at another table who's peacefully sipping from their mug (#337).

#118

After a few minutes' walk on the cobblestone road, you hear the clamor of the marketplace clearly, as if it were just a few steps away.

You can continue north along the road (#359).

Or you can turn south and enter 📖**Housmins** from this road (#394).

#119

"Never heard of her! What business would any stranger have here?!" the guards grumble.

It's clear you won't get anywhere with them. If Kiena was ever here or is still around, these fools know nothing about her.

"I just want to look around the city. I've heard a lot about the Citadel." (#249)

Or you can simply bypass them and enter the city (#59).

#120

The guards cross their spears in front of you, making it immediately clear that you won't get into 📖Moonward this way.

It seems you'll need to find another way to enter the city.

For now, you can head south along a narrower path between the houses, following the city wall (#238), or you can go west, following the road through the forest (#297).

#121

The corridor begins to rise, and after a few steps, it continues into an upward staircase. You can't describe how uplifting it feels to walk out of the mud.

The staircase turns sharply to the left, then, after a few more steps, abruptly ends. You don't even reach the end, as you can see the passage simply wasn't continued from here. It's possible more chambers will be carved out later, but for now, there's no sign of such work.

With a sour expression, you realize the only way forward is back. You walk down the stairs, take a deep breath, and return to the familiar knee-deep mud (#4).

#122

You cut straight across to the other side of the marketplace and continue your journey. The houses soon disappear from the roadside, and you find yourself in a world of wheat fields. The path to the mill isn't long, but it's clear why it was built so far out — this seems to be the highest point in the area, where the wind is strongest, when it blows.

Fortunately, there's hardly any wind now, though the mill's sails keep turning slowly.

You see no one around, and the mill's door stands wide open (#193).

#123

You continue your journey along the wide stone road, the trees growing denser around you, and it seems the path will lead through a forest. Soon, you're walking in the middle of a shaded road, covered by trees and foliage, with no one else in sight for now. Only the gentle sounds of nature surround you.

You're likely near the heart of the forest, as you can see the trees thinning out to the north and south along the road.

You can head north (#244).

Or you can go south (#343).

#124

You admire the maps, marveling at their intricate detail, but you honestly admit that you don't recognize most of them, even with the city names written below. Not all maps depict streets — some show underground tunnels or sewer systems.

The only map that catches your eye is one of 🗺️**Whitpoint**, specifically its hidden streets, oddly tucked behind house firewalls or fences. It seems like a useful little map, especially since that's where you're headed.

You take the 🧺🗺️**Whitpoint map (2-9-7)** off the wall and carefully roll it up to store it.

If you'd like, you can examine the books to see if you find anything interesting there too (#350).

Or, if you're ready to leave, there's one exit, a door leading back to the smoking room (#386).

#125

Youngrek is not only a skilled blacksmith but also knowledgeable about the weapons he crafts.

He praises your choice, saying he couldn't have recommended a better one himself. He explains that every weapon he makes is specially balanced to deal maximum damage with minimal effort and speed.

He's happy to show you a few tricks with your chosen weapon, but not for free. If you want, you can pay him **3**⊛ for his advice, which will grant your character **+1**🗡 point. He has plenty of good tips, and if you have enough gold, you can pay him multiple times for additional 🗡 points.

You can also ask him how an outsider like yourself might still get into the city (#170).

If you're ready to move on, you can take the paths behind the houses back toward the harbor and the fish market (#320), follow the city walls toward the Wamake gate (#140), or follow the signposts northwest to 📖**Oceastall** (#99) or southeast to 📖**Moonward** (#363), leaving 📖**Dispel** behind for good.

#126

You pay the gold to Oreth, who shows you the staircase leading to the upper floor where the rooms are. He encourages you to choose whichever you like, noting that the room overlooking the back courtyard is definitely quieter than the one facing the main square.

You walk up the stairs to the upper floor, where two rooms open off the corridor.

You can go to the room overlooking the main square (#210) or choose the one facing the back courtyard (#153).

#127

The person slumbering next to you has completely knocked themselves out, and judging by the smell, a hefty amount of beer is to blame. On the table, there's a plate with a few bites of cheese and roasted meat, which they didn't have the time or inclination to finish.

You also notice that on the side where you're sitting, a small purse hangs from their belt, which you could easily unhook. As they say, opportunity makes the thief, so you slide closer, keeping your hand concealed, and with a quick move, the purse is in your grasp. You carefully open it to check your loot — not bad, **+4✸** has found a new owner in you.

Just as you're about to stand up from the table, you notice three rough-looking figures at a table near a pillar adorned with stag antlers, watching your every move. They likely saw you swipe the purse. They're clearly observing you but say nothing.

Then one of them gestures unmistakably for you to join them at their table.

> If you know 💡**who they are** and what they're scheming, you can sit with them by multiplying the two numbers under the antlers decorating the pillar, adding the result to this chapter's number, and continuing at the resulting chapter.

You can ignore them and walk to the bartender to order something (#195).

You can sit with a lone drinker at another table (#337).

Or, if you've had enough of tavern troubles, you can head back to the city (#143).

#128

You walk toward the girl, who notices your approach, and a large swarm of bees targets you, forcing you to stop. The bees form a dark cloud a few meters between you and the girl but don't come closer.

Beneath the radiant sun, its golden rays streaming through the sprawling branches of ancient oaks, you stand before the young girl, your voice calm and earnest as you introduce yourself again, assuring her of your peaceful intentions. The air vibrates with the lively hum of bees, and the sweet fragrance of wildflowers and fresh honey dances in the warm breeze. She hesitates, her wide eyes — framed by tousled auburn hair — scanning you with a blend of wariness and curiosity, catching the sunlight in flecks of hazel. After a moment, her posture softens, and a shy smile curves her lips. "I'm Angene," she says gently, her voice carrying the soft lilt of the countryside. "This is my farm. I care for the hives and gather honey here — it's been my family's way for generations."

Captivated by the remarkable scene you've just witnessed, you voice your amazement, admitting you've never seen anyone guide animals with such natural ease. "What kind of magic lets you do that?" you ask, your tone brimming with wonder. Angene's expression shifts, a shadow of doubt crossing her sunlit face as she glances at the hives, where bees weave intricate patterns in the bright daylight. She shakes her head, her fingers nervously twisting the hem of her pale linen dress. "I don't truly know why it happens," she admits, her voice barely above a whisper. "It began one ordinary morning. I was at an old stone altar in the woods nearby, offering prayers for a bountiful harvest, as I always did. Out of nowhere, a strange warmth wrapped around me, like sunlight pouring into my soul. At first, I thought it was... perhaps a divine blessing, or even the warmth of love itself."

Her gaze drifts, lost in the memory, as she continues. "But when the sensation faded, the world felt... transformed. The air pulsed with life, and I could sense the animals' thoughts, like soft murmurs in my mind. I could guide them without speaking." A flicker of pain darkens her features, and her voice quavers. "Then panic struck. A sudden, terrible fear overwhelmed me — I knew something had happened to my father. He was working the fields, and this awful certainty gripped me that he was in peril. I fled from the altar, heart racing, tears stinging my eyes as I stumbled through the sun-dappled undergrowth."

Abruptly, Angene stops, her eyes falling to the ground where vibrant wild grasses sway in the gentle breeze, kissed by the sun's warmth. The deep sorrow etched into her face feels almost tangible, a heavy grief that lingers in the golden stillness of the farm. The bees' steady hum weaves a soft, melancholic undertone, as if echoing her unspoken pain, leaving you with a quiet empathy for this enigmatic young woman and the mysterious gift that has reshaped her life beneath the bright, unyielding light of day.

If you've heard 💡**a story about Angene from someone else before**, you can share it with her by adding the two numbers together, then adding that sum to this chapter's number, and continuing from there.

Of course, you might not have anything to say, and it could be time to set off on your own adventure (#31).

#129

Have you examined the statue before?

If this is your first time (#341), or if you've already examined it (#247).

#130

You've been wandering in the forest for a while when you spot a signpost pointing north toward 📖**Moonward**. To the east, you see trampled flowers leading into the dense forest.

You can follow the signpost north (#39).

Or head in the opposite direction, continuing south along the road (#271).

You can follow the trampled flowers (#213).

#131

This room feels familiar; you've been here before.

It seems there's still nothing interesting to find here.

You can pass through an arched opening to another very similar room (#295), or leave this chamber via a smaller corridor to the northwest (#326).

#132

You sprint down the main street, where the crowd isn't too dense for you to blend in easily.

The guards are hot on your heels.

You can turn left into the side streets (#68) or continue forward along the main street (#377).

#133

The rusty key indeed opens the lock; Knireek's efforts with the guard weren't in vain. You push aside the grated sewer opening and quickly and gracefully climb down the ladder. Once your head is below ground, you carefully pull the sewer cover back over the opening to avoid anyone noticing someone was here.

At the bottom of the ladder, several more steps lead downward.

You're deep underground when the steps finally run out beneath your feet (#46).

#134

You wander through the dense forest, spotting white flowers to your left and a few freshly cut trunks to your right.

You can go left (#324) or right (#78).

#135

You carefully make your way along the rest of the path, but you don't have a good strategy to fend off the bees, and you suffer a few stings, costing you **-3**⚡ points. Still, you reach the house's entrance, where, after a quick knock, the door opens a crack, revealing two curious eyes.

You explain that you're a traveler searching for someone named Kiena. The owner of the eyes shakes their head, saying they've never heard of anyone by that name. You assure them you mean no harm and just want to rest a bit before moving on, if they'd allow it.

The person tells you to make yourself at home outside and rest as long as you need before continuing, then shuts the door in your face (#233).

#136

You recognize this small chamber; it feels a bit like you're going in circles around the same area, but at least you now know where the traps are and can carefully avoid them.

Two paths lead out of this room: one branch of the tunnel system continues north (#234), or you can pass through an arched opening into another similar chamber (#183).

#137

You wander through the dense forest, spotting white flowers to your left.

You can go left (#367) or right (#324).

#138

With a warm wave and a heartfelt smile, you call out your thanks to Kokary for his generous hospitality, his weathered face crinkling with a nod of acknowledgment. You turn to join the small, cheerful group of villagers, their faces aglow with welcoming grins as they eagerly beckon you to follow them toward the granary. The path winds through the heart of the village, a short jaunt roughly equal to the distance from the bustling marketplace to the old stone mill — but on the opposite side, where quaint thatched-roof houses nestle amid vibrant wildflower patches and sun-dappled greenery. The air hums with the earthy scent of freshly turned soil and the faint sweetness of blooming honeysuckle, carried on a gentle breeze.

As you walk, you idly ponder the curious placement of the granary, wondering why the villagers didn't build it closer to the mill for convenience. The thought drifts like a passing cloud, overshadowed by the charm of the journey. Soon, the granary comes into view, a striking structure crafted with meticulous care. Its sturdy timber walls gleam with a warm, honeyed hue under the midday sun, and a neatly woven reed fence encircles it, the intricate patterns of the reeds catching the light like delicate golden threads. Nearby, a handful of chickens strut and peck at the soft earth, their feathers flashing iridescent shades of russet and gold, suggesting the area might occasionally serve as a pen for small livestock like sheep or goats. The scene is a vivid tapestry of rural life, vibrant and serene, inviting you to pause and take in the quiet beauty of this well-loved village corner.

If this is your first time at the festival (#255), or if you've been here before (#67).

#139

The bookstore seems like a quiet place, though it's clear this town isn't a cultural hub, and this spot is definitely not the busiest place in the city.

If this is your first time here (#185), or if you've been here before (#236).

#140

You slowly approach the city's grand gate, which you quickly learned the locals call the Wamake Gate, modestly named after one of their ancient kings. You must admit, the gate is a stunning piece of craftsmanship, carved from stone with intricate detail, paying fitting tribute to their late ruler. The two massive towers flanking the gate are equally impressive, and you've heard they symbolize the king's two consorts and one child from each consort. Regardless, the sight is well worth admiring.

The sculptural patterns show signs of wear from time, but that doesn't diminish the gate's breathtaking beauty. Beside the gate, three or four armored guards chat and occasionally laugh, wielding massive halberds – not the kind of people you'd want to cross.

The path into the city leads through the gate (#30), but you can also hear the bustle of the marketplace (#181), where you're sure you could buy food or clothing.

In the direction of the river, you see the signs of a few small workshops (#77).

#141

"Where did you get these valuable items?" one of them asks.

"I found them," you say simply, prompting a laugh from another.

"My friend, in our line of work, we don't find things — we acquire them," he says, patting your shoulder approvingly. "I can't imagine what you went through to get these, but I suspect it wasn't purely your noble heart that led you here."

You nod reluctantly, admitting it's true.

"Let's make a deal," he proposes. "There's a wealthy house (5-25) here, full of valuable items. What we're after is a golden statue. If you bring us that statue here, we'll pay you handsomely, and then we all go our separate ways. What do you say?"

You nod, indicating it sounds like a solid deal and that you'll think it over.

"Don't think too long — we're leaving tomorrow," he says, patting your shoulder again.

It's an interesting offer, but you can't promise or say much more.

You give his shoulder an encouraging pat, bid him farewell, and consider your options: you can head to the tavern across the square (#216), leave the bustle for the harbor to the southwest (#96), or follow the narrower street behind the platform to the northeast (#387).

#142

You walk to the end of the corridor, where you see only narrow tunnels branching in two directions. You step over the grated door previously laid on the ground, deciding which way to go next.

You can head back south along the ornate corridor (#101).

You can crawl into the tunnel to the east (#198).

You can crawl into the tunnel to the west (#239).

#143

You step out of the tavern and look around to decide where to go next.

You can head toward the Citadel (#41) or leave the city through the Wamake gate (#149).

You can linger here for a bit and look around, hoping to spot something interesting (#69).

If you've had enough of the fresh air, you can go back into the tavern (#113).

#144

You ask the locals to let you climb the ladder, and they pause their work for a few minutes. You can see they're working hard to clear the granary as quickly as possible.

You give them a friendly wave and walk back toward the village, passing the familiar wheat fields. Behind you, you hear them resume their work, sounding as though they're working even harder than before.

You stride steadily toward the village's main street (#394).

#145

You sneak out onto the small street and from there head toward the main street (#169).

#146

The traditional pews have nothing special about them. You inspect one of the piles stacked against the wall at random, but you don't find anything truly useful. These pews are only good for firewood now.

You can check out the altar if you haven't already (#311).

Or, if you've seen enough, you can head back north through the corridor (#101).

#147

You carefully pull out the bottle, and the group erupts in loud cheers, clearly making you an honorary member for successfully getting the wine from the bartender.

One of them pulls the cork from the bottle and pours a generous amount for everyone. You start drinking and laughing together, and as long as the wine lasts, you feel great – add **+2 ⚡** points to yourself.

Feeling a bit woozy after several glasses, you decide to step outside for some fresh air before deciding what to do next (#348).

#148

Every nerve in your body is coiled tight, your breath caught in your throat as you fixate on the trembling bush. A faint rustle sharpens your senses, heart pounding. Then, a small rabbit creeps out from the shadowed leaves, its eyes glinting in the dim light.

It barely notices you, nibbling at the ground, but the slightest twitch of your foot sends it bolting in panic, a blur of fur vanishing into the dense, whispering grass across the path.

That went easily (#73).

#149

You slowly approach the city's grand gate, known to the locals as the Wamake Gate. It's an impressive sight, even from the inner side.

You walk calmly toward the gate, and the guards, laughing among themselves, pay you no mind, allowing you to stroll out beyond the gate.

From here, you can go in several directions: back into the inner city through the gate (#30), or toward the clamor of the marketplace (#181), where you can surely buy food and clothing.

In the direction of the river, you see the signs of a few small work-shops (#77).

#150

You place the gold on the counter and order a pint of the local beer. The bartender, Freela, gives you a playful smile, sizes you up, and pockets the gold. You take a sip of the beer — it's surprisingly good, worth its price. Add **+1**⚡ point to yourself.

"Just call for Freela if you need anything," the fairy tosses out after tucking away your gold.

You've heard that line a thousand times before and silently acknowledge her words with a bored grimace, taking another big gulp of the beer.

As she turns away to go about her business, you call after her.

"Hey, Freela!" you beckon her back.

She walks over to you, waiting expectantly for what you want.

> If you have 💡**a bouquet of flowers**, you can give it to her by adding the two numbers together, adding that sum to this chapter's number, and continuing your reading there.
>
> If you have 💡**a vial of potion**, you can give it to her by adding the two numbers together, adding that sum to this chapter's number, and continuing your reading there.

You can ask about Kiena (#97).

You can ask about local gossip (#260).

#151

Jarse tells you that recently, several people have tried to rob the Citadel in 📖 **Dispel**, and a few managed to take some valuable items. The guards are trying to catch these thieves or at least make their job harder.

You ask what was stolen from the Citadel, but Jarse can't say exactly. He does know, however, that multiple incidents occurred in recent days, which is why there's such heightened security. He mentions that Oreth, the local tavern keeper, isn't happy about the ban on outsiders entering the city, as the locals bring little gold to his business.

Beyond that, he doesn't know much about the thefts. It's possible the thieves are hiding in the nearby forests temporarily, waiting for the guard presence to ease before continuing their journey — who knows.

You ask if he's heard anything about such elusive bandit groups, but he shakes his head, saying only that a wizard named Nold Syanka lives in the forest and might know more, if the rumors are true. When you ask where to find the wizard, he can't pinpoint the location of the hut, only that it's somewhere in the forests south of 📖 **Moonward**. No one knows the exact path, as it's as if the wizard changes their hideout's location from time to time to avoid being found, he says with a shrug.

You can ask him kindly what he's doing here exactly (#11), or inquire about Kiena, as he might know or have heard something (#273).

From here, you can also move on in two directions between the houses: north (#39) or west, following the city wall (#238).

#152

You start down the corridor, which abruptly ends without any warning. There's nothing at the end of the corridor — it simply doesn't continue.

You scratch your head and head back the way you came (#87).

#153

The room overlooks the back courtyard, which looks like a small fortress with its high fenced walls.

> If you know 💡**where the bartender keeps the wine**, you can get there by subtracting the smaller number from the larger one, adding the result to this chapter's number, and continuing there.

If you just want to rest a bit (#389).

#154

The door opens silently, clearly leading to a dining room where a massive handcrafted chandelier hangs from the ceiling. The table is set for a light afternoon meal, and you quickly count ten place settings as you inspect the silver cutlery. In the center of the table stands a large vase filled with a fresh bouquet of flowers.

> You hear noises and voices from upstairs — you're not alone in the house! Roll two dice. If the result is higher than your 🖋 points, you unfortunately failed to stay silent and unnoticed; continue the story here (#13).

If this is your first time here (#90), or if you've been here before (#318).

#155

You head toward the carpenter's workshop.

If this is your first time here (#19), or if you've been here before (#58).

#156

The road leads straight to the city gate, where two stern guards stand vigilantly. Ivy climbs haphazardly up the walls beside the gate, yet it creates a pleasant, welcoming sight, almost inviting every visitor to enter the city and rest.

You can try walking into the city past the guards (#120).

> If you have ♀**a vial of essential oil**, you can use it here by multiplying the two numbers, subtracting the result from this chapter's number, and continuing your reading there.

Or you can head south along a narrower path between the houses, following the city wall (#238).

Alternatively, you can follow the road west through the forest (#297).

#157

You leave the marketplace and, heading back along the main street, soon find yourself on the dirt road leading toward 📖**Dispel**. A few clouds momentarily block the sun, but it seems they'll pass in minutes, revealing the sun again from behind their fluffy cover.

As you approach the city, the golden wheat fields gradually thin out, and though you can't yet see Youngrek's blacksmith workshop in the distance, the gently swaying crops have already disappeared from the roadside.

In the distance, the city's outlines slowly come into sharper focus (#220).

#158

The trees and bushes grow denser around you, and soon the path leads through the heart of the forest. For now, you see nothing on the road, neither nearby nor in the distance.

You can continue west (#84) or head east (#355).

#159

The narrow path is lined with trees and bushes, and it doesn't take long before it widens slightly and reaches a small junction.

At the junction's signpost, you see that north leads to 📖**Houdmins** village, east points toward Dig city, and west, just a few minutes' walk away, you can make out the outlines of 📖**Whitpoint** city.

You can head toward 📖**Houdmins** (#347), take the eastern path toward Dig as indicated by the sign (#91), or make 📖**Whitpoint** your next stop (#290).

#160

This tunnel is narrower than any before, a miracle you can even crawl forward. It slopes steeply upward for a while, then sharply turns, almost doubling back, though you can't be sure — it's just a gut feeling in this blind darkness.

Complete darkness surrounds you, and breathing becomes harder in the damp, confined space. You pause to slow your breathing, but it's tough. This short tunnel journey drains your energy, costing you **-2**⚡ points.

It's hard to shake the fear that the tunnel might abruptly end, forcing you to crawl back, or worse, collapse behind you, trapping you forever. But luckily, after countless turns, you spot a faint pinpoint of light in the distance.

The light grows stronger as you crawl closer, and soon there's no doubt — this tunnel leads straight to the Citadel's basement. Just a few dozen meters more, and you're there.

Relieved, you find the other end of the tunnel isn't blocked; it simply opens into a small chamber (#87).

#161

The guards cross their spears in front of you, and you immediately realize you won't easily get into 📖**Moonward**. One of them mutters something about "scram, stranger" and prods you with the blunt end of his spear, gently but firmly enough to knock you to the ground, costing you **-1**⚡ point.

You stand up, brush off your clothes, and size up the guards. There are two of them — maybe you have a chance to get past them and restore your wounded pride in one go. If you think it's worth confronting them, it's time to draw your weapon and show them how things are done (#312).

If you decide it's not worth the effort, you can head south along a narrower path between the houses, following the city wall (#356), or east back toward the river and the small bridge crossing it (#39).

#162

He sits down beside the anvil, wiping his forehead, and asks how he can help you today.

You can ask about Kiena, in case he's heard of her (#298).

You can inquire about the weapons he's currently working on (#86).

Or you can set off, heading north along a path from here (#156), or west, following the city wall (#356).

#163

The tunnel keeps narrowing as you move forward until you reach a T-junction. Light filters down from somewhere above, illuminating the junction, but you can't see the source of the light. Overall, there's nothing here except the damp tunnel walls.

From here, a continuous corridor leads north (#105) and south (#234), while the shorter branch of the junction heads east (#23).

#164

You leave the main street and head toward the wheat fields, where you see villagers working diligently in the distance. As you get closer and overhear their conversation, it becomes clear that this is their underground granary, currently covered in muddy, watery sludge. They need to clean it out before the real harvest begins, or they'll have nowhere to store the wheat — hence the many buckets they're tirelessly carrying up from the granary.

You ask if you can go down to the granary. They tell you they've only partially cleared the mud from the first chamber, and the other rooms might still be completely impassable or at least difficult to access.

If you decide you don't want to go down yet and prefer to walk back to the main street and head to the tavern (#394).

If you ask them to let you climb down the ladder to the granary (#102).

#165

You take out the basket of fish, and you can immediately tell from the villagers' gestures that you won't get any gold for it here.

If you still want to offer the 🧺**large basket of fish** to save the festival for free (#274).

Or you can leave this awkward situation as quickly as possible and walk back through the houses to the marketplace (#6).

#166

You place the **5**✹ on the table without blinking, and Jarse, with fitting politeness, slips them into his pockets (#230).

#167

In the recess, you see a corridor blocked by a grated door, while the passage also continues east, though you can't see its end from here.

The small, cozy recess's grated door definitely demands attention, as beyond the bars, you see a much wider corridor lined with colorful stones, seemingly leading toward a larger room. You can't quite make out what awaits there, but it's certainly more inviting than the narrow tunnel you're currently forced to crawl through.

Upon examining the grated door, you notice a sturdy lock, but as far as you know, you don't have a key that fits it.

You can try pulling the grated door toward you (#399).

You can try pushing the grated door (#287).

#168

You're standing in a small chamber.

> The mud reaches up to your knees, making it very difficult and unsteady to move forward. You slip and stumble, barely managing to keep your balance. Roll two dice, and if the resulting number is greater than your 🏃 points, deduct **-1**⚡ from yourself as you trip in the mud, fall, and suffer a minor injury.

From this chamber, you can head left through a short corridor to another room (#378).

Or you can pass through a small opening in the wall to a much larger chamber (#308).

#169

You walk among the houses on the city's widest street, the neat little homes signaling prosperity. You continue along the road until you reach a Y-shaped junction, where the path splits in three directions. To the east and northeast, you see two small bridges, both crossing the Shorough River.

If you've heard of 💡**the wealthy house**, you can find it by multiplying the two numbers, adding the result to this chapter's number, and continuing there.

You can go west from here (#355), or cross the river in two directions: northeast (#96) or east (#276).

#170

Youngrek kindly explains that you're not the only one who wants to enter the city, but the guards don't allow strangers through the main gate. However, there's a small grated opening in the wall between the outer houses, its lock currently broken, and you might be able to sneak inside the inner walls through it.

He draws you a map showing where to find the grated opening in the stone wall among the houses and huts, marking it clearly with two numbers: 2-7.

The drawing seems clear to you, and as you look at it, it appears easy to find.

You carefully put the map away.

You can take the paths behind the houses back toward the harbor in the direction of the fish market (#320), or follow the city walls toward the Wamake gate (#140), or follow the signposts northwest to 🗺️**Oceastall** (#99), or southeast to 🗺️**Moonward** (#363).

#171

You take out the potion and hand the vial to Freela.

"What a noble gesture from you, stranger!" she says, taking the vial and carefully pulling out the tiny cork. You're just about to realize this might not be a good idea, but it's too late. Purple vapor envelops you instantly, lulling you into a deep sleep. You collapse, snoring peacefully, in the middle of the tavern.

> You don't know exactly how long you were unconscious, but as you start to come to, you realize you're no longer in the tavern but in one of the back streets. You quickly reach for your purse, only to find all your gold stolen (reset it to zero now).

You check your other possessions — luckily, nothing else is missing except the small vial that held the potion, which Freela has likely claimed for herself. Your head still feels a bit foggy, and you decide to take revenge on Freela for this, but as your mind clears, you're not sure it was intentional. Why she threw you out of the tavern remains another question, but you're not particularly interested in the answer right now.

Finding Kiena is your top priority at this moment.

You gather yourself, stand up, brush off your clothes, and head back to the village's main street (#394).

#172

As you approach the table, two skeletons suddenly rise from behind it and advance toward you.

There's not much you can do now — it's time to draw your weapon.

Skeleton #1 (with Sword)	13⚡4🗡 ⊙4→|←2🛡
Skeleton #2 (with Sword)	17⚡5🗡 ⊙3→|←1🛡

If you defeat the skeletons, you can now walk over to the table and examine the leftovers.

Most of the food is rotten or moldy, but in the fruit bowl, you find a few green apples that still seem edible. If you want, you can take the 🧺**green apples** with you; eating them will grant you **+3⚡** points.

There's not much else to see at the table. If you wish, you can head northeast through a small opening to another chamber (#263), or continue through a corridor leading northwest in the room's far wall (#191).

#173

The other book you received from Pap is a much friendlier one about local legends, written in Fop language, which is best known for its pictorial representations, featuring arched motifs made up of semi-circles or full circles.

It's quite easy to read — and just as easy to misinterpret. The legend of the Blue Moon traces back to the pens of the first settlers, seemingly recorded with a scientific intent.

T he Effect of the Blue Moon

In the northern parts of the island, it's observed during every solstice ~ twice a year ~ that the Moon turns blue at night. This effect is visible for approximately two or three nights.

The light's influence is quite beneficial for the harvest; if the sky is clear and no icy lightning obscures the Moon, the yield becomes abundant and flavorful. Very rarely, when the Moon's full light illuminates the hills for all three nights, the chole Gemoon Chemn grapes ripen to their sweetest. This grape is famously the base for the justly renowned imperial-level dispeli ruby wine.

When such a harvest can be reaped, even the ruler occasionally visits from Winwel to purchase the finest wines for the royal family.

The last such clear, blue-moon-lit sky was observed only generations ago.

The Blue Moon's beneficial effect on crops is offset by its negative impact on animals. It's noted that the Blue Moon's light drives animals into a frenzy, causing them to attack each other without any apparent reason, regardless of whether the light is visible or hidden behind clouds.

During this period, it's not advisable to spend the night in the wild, as the frenzied animals spare no one. However, it was an ancient tradition for a boy's rite of passage to spend a night under the Blue Moon's light, and if he returned the next day, he was declared a warrior.

In modern times, such traditions are no longer followed, though many thrill-seekers still pay homage to these ancient customs ~ and few of them return.

The book is interesting but mainly focuses on the Blue Moon and the experiences accumulated over generations, offering nothing particularly noteworthy. You close the book and place it on top of one of the stacks.

Would you like to read about 📖 **Dispel's** history (#38)?

Would you like to read about the Citadel (#114)?

Or have you had enough of legends and prefer to leave the bookstore for now (#77)?

#174

You explain that you're searching for some magical stones and are certain Kiena can help you find them, which is why you want to catch up with her as soon as possible.

The woodcutter laughs, saying it's obvious Kiena might be after the stones too, as he met her in the forest two days ago. You ask what Kiena was doing there, but he can't tell you. You try to enthusiastically and friendly describe the magical stones you're seeking, but the woodcutters have had too much to drink to fully grasp your story. One of them finally says that, whatever the case, if you're heading into the forest, don't follow the white flowers, as they'll only get you into trouble.

You can ask them about the forests around the city (#184).

Or, if that doesn't interest you, you can talk to the bartender instead (#281).

If you'd like to leave the tavern and return to the main square, you can do that too (#348).

#175

You enter a smaller central chamber, which likely served as a small guard post at the entrance to the corridor leading to the prison cells at some point. The table and chairs are half-rotted, but the keys to the cells still hang on the wall.

If you'd like to examine the keys (#10).

You can also continue southeast toward the cells (#280).

There are two other exits from the room: a longer corridor leads northwest (#288), and through a smaller passage to the northeast, you can see another larger chamber (#376).

#176

You wipe your forehead after the sweaty work and wave goodbye to Ifer. He waves back enthusiastically, clearly showing how much he appreciated your help.

Halfway out, you notice the glove he gave you is still on your hand; he didn't mention taking it off, and now you decide not to turn back for it. Instead, you choose to keep the 🧺 0=0 **leather glove**. It fits you comfortably and suits your hand perfectly, granting you **+2 0=0** points during combat as long as you have it.

With a small sense of satisfaction on your face, you step out onto the street (#77).

#177

You take out the yellow flowers and approach the altar with them.

As you get closer, the altar begins to glow more intensely with an otherworldly blue light, and the nearer you try to get, the harder it feels to step forward. The mysterious blue light firmly keeps you at a distance from the altar.

Holding the flowers out in front of you, you attempt to approach, and surprisingly, the blue light allows you to get close enough to place the bouquet on the altar. You set the yellow flowers down.

You can try to take the blue flowers (#7).

Or you can step away from the altar respectfully (#71).

#178

"Thirty gold," you repeat firmly.

Knireek locks eyes with you, and for a few moments that feel endless, you size each other up. The tension in the air is palpable, destined to break one way or another in mere seconds.

"Twenty-five," says Knireek.

"Twenty-eight," you counter immediately.

"Twenty-seven!" Knireek slams the table.

Twenty-seven, you nod, and slide the pouch containing the stone closer to him, signaling that the deal is settled from your side. Knireek unhooks another pouch from his belt, opens it, and counts out seven more gold pieces on the table alongside the original twenty.

Knireek's companion, who had stabbed a dagger into the table, puts the knife away. You tear off another piece of roast, and now you eat together in complete peace, which grants you **+2 ⚡** points.

You linger a bit longer with Knireek and his crew, chatting about various topics and having a few drinks.

Before you stand up and leave the tavern (#143), don't forget to take your well-deserved **27 ☀**.

#179

The map's precise instructions for pressing the stones send a chill down your spine, each touch feeling like a dare against some unseen force. When the door grinds open with a low, guttural groan, your pulse quickens. You step into a chamber that reeks of ancient decay, unmistakably a burial vault. Ornate blue crests gleam faintly on the walls, their intricate patterns seeming to pulse in the flickering torch-light. At the room's heart looms a stone coffin, its four sturdy legs rooted to the floor like silent sentinels. The air grows heavier, the eerie stillness of the haunted basement pressing against your chest, as if the chamber itself is watching, waiting.

You can examine the crests on the wall (#221).

You can try to open the coffin (#267).

Or you can leave the room (#45).

#180

You slip through the door into a cramped chamber, the floor sloping unevenly toward the far wall, a telltale sign of the earth's slow, ancient shift. Your torchlight dances across the shadows, revealing a stout oak door on the opposite side, its iron bands glinting defiantly. But where the chamber sags, dark water pools, swallowing the door's base. The iron reinforcements vanish into the murky depths below and bite into the ceiling above, anchoring it against time's pull. Your heart races as you edge closer, the cold water lapping at your boots, daring you to wade into the unknown to pry open the next stage of your quest.

It's certain that opening this door won't be easy.

You can return to the room you came from (#263).

You can try ramming it with your shoulder to force it open (#94).

If you have a sword, you can attempt to pry the door open near the bands (#325).

#181

The marketplace buzzes even more intensely as you stand beside it. It seems you've hit the busiest time — everyone wants to sell, and each claims to have the best prices in the city.

You might find something here that could be useful to you.

If you have a 🧺**large basket of fish**, you can try to sell it here for **5**⊛.

If you have a 🧺**bundle of wheat**, you can try to sell it here for **8**⊛.

If you have a 🧺**sack of flour**, you can try to sell it here for **12**⊛.

If you have a 🧺**leather glove**, you can try to sell it here for **13**⊛.

You can buy a 🧺**roll of rope** here for **2**⊛.

You can buy a 🧺 ⫘**thick hooded cloak** here for **5**⊛; this cloak grants **+1**⫘ as long as you have it and use it.

You can buy a 🧺**basket of apples** here for **3**⊛; consuming all these apples will grant you **+5**⚡ points.

You can buy a 🧺 ⫘**vial of elixir** here for **7**⊛; consuming this elixir during your current battle will grant you **+5**⫘. You can use it once, don't forget to remove it after that.

Once you've finished shopping, you can continue toward the inner city along the road to the Wamake gate (#140), or head back to the harbor (#1), or explore around the small workshop signs in the distance (#77).

#182

You peer through the grimy window, its warped glass framing the challenge below, your mind racing as you plot your daring escape. A faint chill seeps through the frame, carrying the scent of damp wood and earth. Beyond the sill, the slanted roof of a weathered shed juts out, its shingles cracked and moss-streaked, promising a precarious foothold. From there, your gaze drops to a stout wooden barrel in the backyard, its iron hoops rusted but sturdy, standing amidst over-grown grass and scattered debris. A leap to the barrel could deliver you to the soft, uneven ground of the yard, where shadows pool under gnarled trees, but one misstep on the shed's slick roof could send you crashing. Your fingers grip the splintered window frame, heart thudding as you weigh the risky descent against the urgent need to move forward.

> As you jump off the barrel, you lose your balance and fall. You don't suffer serious harm, but deduct **-2⚡** points from yourself. After that, you stand up and brush yourself off.

From here, a straight path leads to the wine cellar; fortunately, the door isn't locked (#62).

#183

You arrive in a room with a floor adorned with ornate stones. You glance around quickly but see nothing particularly special here.

If this is your first time here (#351), or if you've been here before (#131).

#184

You couldn't ask them anything easier — they know the forest like the back of their hand. They've just brought a load of firewood into the city. The cold season is still far off, but they're already earning well from it.

You ask them which forest they work in most, and they tell you it's the southern woods, on the other side of the river, where the forest is densest and where they've found the finest oaks so far. They enthusiastically describe the beautiful logs they've cut there. Laughing, they say many more sturdy trunks will soon feel the bite of their axes.

They recount how, while chopping wood deeper into the forest, they stumbled upon a foreboding hut with bluish-purple smoke rising from its chimney — likely the lair of some wizard or demon. When they saw it, they turned back immediately. Fortunately, no major misfortune befell them, but they're certain to give that place a wide berth in the future.

You can ask them if they've heard of Kiena (#393).

Or, if that doesn't interest you, you can talk to the bartender instead (#281).

#185

You step into the bookstore and notice as you look around that organization is definitely not the owner's strong suit. Books are stacked in piles in the corners, on shelves, on the floor, and practically everywhere there's space. The owner greets you courteously and introduces himself as Pap, revealing that he and his ancestors have owned this bookstore for generations.

He occasionally travels to collect new books from all over the kingdom. He assures you that you're lucky to find him here, as he's preparing for a longer trip to the capital, 📖**Winwel**, in the coming days to bring back more treasures.

You can ask Pap about anything specific that interests you; he's sure to have a book on it (#236).

Or you can leave the books for now and explore something else outside (#77).

#186

You stand at the door of the chamber, unable to go much farther because the room beyond is submerged in water. You can't tell exactly how deep it is, and the water looks terribly murky.

It's not out of the question that there might be some kind of secret passage beneath the water, so it might be worth investigating what's under there (#206).

If you want to leave the room, you have two options: a narrow corridor leads southeast from here (#277), and through an opening to the east, you can see another chamber that appears to contain some kind of altar, as far as you can make out from here (#365).

#187

The coffin lid is already open, and there's not much new to find here.

You can also examine the crests on the wall (#221), or leave the room the way you came (#45).

#188

You're in a dark, slightly narrower section of the tunnel, mostly feeling your way along the wall with your hand and taking small steps because you can't see what's underfoot. So far, you're lucky — the ground is a bit damp but completely smooth.

You can continue north, where some light is filtering in (#23).

Or you can go south, where the stairs are (#46).

#189

You place the gold on the table and slowly unfasten your armor to allow Mog easier access to your wounds. Your injuries are quite severe, but Mog knows his craft. Each ointment feels like a divine touch, and the fatigue and pain fade so quickly it's as if they were never there.

You chat while he works, discussing local customs. He mentions there's a big event happening in the city, which isn't ideal for an old man like him. You also ask about Kiena, but he hasn't heard anything about her. He encourages you to check the tavern or the harbor, where you might learn more about your friend.

He carefully bandages your wounds, then lets you reattach your armor and continue on your way.

> If you had any serious injuries from before, all their negative effects are gone, and you gain **+2** 🦵 and **+4** ⚡ points.

You feel refreshed and rejuvenated, ready to continue your search for Kiena (#322).

#190

The bartender shakes his head, saying there's no local event being celebrated — just that the fishermen have returned to the city, and a successful catch always fills the tavern and the lantern-lit houses to the brim, depending on what anyone needs.

You nod in agreement.

Bukatiz explains that most of the current crowd are fishermen or work on fishing boats, and he knows many of them by name. However, there are quite a few unfamiliar faces, like yours, which he hasn't seen before, though most here are mostly harmless.

You can ask about local gossip (#117).

You can inquire about the less harmless strangers (#14).

Or, if you're done questioning the bartender, you can sit at a quiet table where someone is already slumped over, fast asleep (#212), or join someone at another table who's peacefully sipping from their mug (#337).

#191

You stand at the corridor's end, where a narrow, jagged opening beckons you toward a vast, shadowy chamber. The air grows thick with the musty scent of ancient stone and secrets. On the western wall, your torchlight catches a cluster of stones, their peculiar arrangement — crooked and mismatched — hinting at a hidden door. Your fingers trace the rough edges, pulse quickening as you sense the promise of untold mysteries beyond. One wrong move could trigger a trap, but the thrill of discovery urges you to press on, ready to unravel the enigma carved into the wall.

If you have 💡**a map of the tower**, you can try to find the secret passage by multiplying the two numbers on the map, subtracting the result from this chapter's number, and continuing there.

Of course, if you prefer, you can head back southeast (#396).

Or you can crawl through the small opening to see what's inside (#279).

#192

The door opens silently, clearly leading into a study room. A large oak table stands here, covered with various papyrus sheets and scrolls that appear to be unfinished works — possibly maps. Piles of rolled-up paper are stacked in the corner. On the opposite wall, there's a cozy little fireplace, currently unlit.

> You hear noises and voices from upstairs — you're not alone in the house! Roll two dice. If the result is higher than your 🖊 points, you unfortunately failed to stay silent and unnoticed; continue the story here (#13).

There are two exits from the room: one through the wall opposite the fireplace (#64), and the other straight ahead (#52).

#193

You're inside the mill, and no one is here; the work seems to be running on its own, with the millstones moving slowly as they grind. Or rather, they're not grinding anything right now — the stones scrape against each other with a hungry screech.

If you have a 🧺 **bundle of wheat**, you can grind it here anytime and take a 🧺 **sack of flour** in exchange.

However, there's not much to see.

You can leave the mill and walk back to the village marketplace (#63).

Or you can leave the mill and cut through the wheat fields to head back toward 🗺 **Dispel** (#331).

#194

You lean closer to Angene, the firelight casting wild shadows across her weathered barn, and recount the tale you overheard in a raucous tavern, where a stranger – claiming to be her lost fiancé – slurred her story through a haze of ale and despair. His eyes, red-rimmed and haunted, gleamed with the pain of a shattered betrothal, his voice breaking as he spoke of a love stolen by fate. Angene's breath catches, her emerald eyes wide with urgency as she presses you for details about this heartbroken wanderer, her voice trembling with hope and dread.

As the conversation unfolds, her words paint vivid images of her father, a formidable wizard cloaked in robes that shimmered like starlit skies. Though Angene shunned the arcane arts, she revered his mastery, his hands weaving spells that crackled with raw power. She swears his final enchantment, cast in his dying moments, wove a protective aura around her, summoning the fierce loyalty of the forest's creatures – wolves with glowing eyes, hawks that soar on silent wings, and even the shimmering beetles that skitter at her feet. Their presence hums with an otherworldly energy, guarding her in this forsaken place.

Her voice softens, tinged with sorrow, as she speaks of arriving at this vibrant village months ago, its cobblestone streets alive with laughter and bustling markets. But a creeping malaise soon descended, a spectral chill that drained the village's color and drove its people away, leaving her alone on this crumbling farm, surrounded by fields of swaying, ghostly wheat. She points south, toward the jagged, mist-shrouded peaks that loom like silent titans, and whispers of the T'lindilhei battlefield (3-35), a cursed expanse where a brutal clash ended in stalemate. The air there, she murmurs, is thick with the restless spirits of fallen warriors, their anguished wails echoing through the valleys, perhaps spilling over to haunt this very village. The distant mountains seem to pulse with an eerie glow, daring you to venture toward the accursed field and uncover its secrets.

Eventually, you shift to other topics. She explains that no spirits have visited her or the farm yet; she's lived here for months, selling honey in nearby small villages and farms for a little gold, which she uses to buy food and clothes. A merchant usually comes after the full moon, reportedly from 📖**Whispel**, where they pay well for honey.

She doesn't encounter travelers, as no one comes to the ghost town of 📖**Kadedh** anymore.

You chat for a while longer, but then bid each other farewell. As a token of her kindness, Angene gives you a 🧺**jar of honey** for the road; if you feel like eating it sometime, it'll grant you **+4⚡** points.

You step out through the small gate of the farm's enclosing fence (#31).

#195

You step up to the tavern counter and beckon the bartender, who gruffly barks that his name is Bukatiz and you can order something if you feel like it.

You can buy a mug of beer here for **1**⊛, which immediately grants **+1**⚡.

You can buy a glass of the famous local purple wine for **2**⊛, which immediately grants **+3**⚡.

You can strike up a conversation with the bartender (#270), or sit at a table with your drink where they're already sleeping it off (#212), or join someone to drink and chat (#337).

If you've had enough of the tavern, you can head back to the city (#143).

#196

Guided by whispered tales, you abandon the road and trace the river's churning waters upstream, its current hissing like a warning against your path toward the cursed battlefield. As you press forward, a suffocating dread coils tighter around your chest, the air growing thick with an unnatural chill that seeps into your bones, a sign you're nearing the haunted killing grounds.

Uncertainty gnaws at you, but the riverbank reveals its grim secrets: skeletal remains of warriors, their armor rusted and splintered, lie tangled among gnarled trees, their empty eye sockets seeming to watch your every step. You push onward, climbing a low, jagged hill, and the full horror of the battlefield sprawls before you.

A desolate expanse stretches to the horizon, littered with shattered skeletons – human and beast alike – strewn amid broken blades and tattered banners. Horses, their bones cracked and splayed, mirror the savagery that claimed their riders. The global scene is frozen in time, two armies locked in their pre-battle lines, facing each other with eerie stillness, as if a malevolent force snuffed them out before the first clash. No victor emerged; instead, a palpable aura of dark magic lingers, its residue staining the air with a faint, sickly shimmer. The restless spirits, bound by this arcane calamity, are said to torment the nearby settlements, their whispers carried on the wind.

Two faded crests stand out amid the carnage: one, ghostly white and gray, bleached by time; the other, a deep blue now dulled to a mournful hue, barely clinging to its former glory. The thought of taking relics from this forsaken place stirs unease – every bone, every shard, hums with the curse's malevolent pulse. Plundering here risks not just your life but your very soul, as the battlefield's wrath spares nothing, living or otherwise.

However, it's definitely worth looking around, as the risk depends on what you might find among the corpses and skeletons.

You can try searching the white-gray crested bodies (#37).

Or the blue-crested ones might seem more interesting (#115).

Of course, you can leave the battlefield in peace before any trouble arises (#269).

#197

You take out the bouquet of yellow flowers and offer it to Freela.

"What's this now? A marriage proposal?!" she laughs loudly.

You're not even sure what you intended, so you shrug, about to say something witty, when Freela continues.

"Look around, stranger. Do you think you can steal my heart with yellow?" she gestures around.

She's right, as your eyes sweep across the tavern's vibrant interior, where the bold hue of sapphire reigns supreme. The heavy curtains draped over the narrow, iron-framed windows shimmer with deep blue velvet, their folds catching the flickering glow of wrought-iron chandeliers suspended from the low, timbered ceiling. Delicate blue ribbons, intricately braided, adorn the edges of sturdy oak tables, their surfaces scarred from years of rowdy patrons. Wreaths of dried lavender and cornflowers, their petals faded to a soft indigo, hang in artful clusters along the rough-hewn stone walls, mingling with the faint scent of woodsmoke and spiced ale that permeates the air.

Freela's auburn hair, loosely tied with a blue cord, glints as she slams tankards onto the counter, her sharp eyes scanning the crowd for trouble. The shelves behind her are lined with clay jugs and pewter mugs, each etched with swirling patterns that echo the tavern's blue motif. Even the worn tapestry above the hearth, depicting a stormy sea with churning waves, weaves shades of cobalt and azure into its threads, tying the room together in a cohesive, almost enchanting palette.

Indeed, yellow has no place in Freela's domain — this tavern pulses with the cool, commanding energy of blue, a reflection of her fierce spirit and unyielding rule over this lively haven.

"But you know what, stranger? If you bring me some nice flowers, I'll tell you a secret," she winks mischievously and leaves you with your beer.

You slowly sip the cool brew, and it's time to decide your next move.

If you'd like to order another mug of the local beer, it will still cost **2⊛** if you have the money for such indulgence (#150).

If you think it's time to leave the tavern, you can do that too (#394).

#198

This branch of the tunnel turns slightly northward, then abruptly ends in a large pile of rubble. At some point, the ceiling must have collapsed, and the debris now completely blocks the passage.

You study it for a while, considering how you might get through, but eventually realize the only way forward is to crawl back through the narrow tunnel (#89).

#199

You stand in front of the tavern, its doors and windows heavily boarded up – there's no chance of getting warm food or a cool drink here today. Around the corner, a group of three people is watching you, trying to figure out what you're up to.

You can leave the village by the road you came in on (#116).

You can try talking to the group of three (#252).

Or you can continue down the main street, hoping to find something interesting (#289).

#200

You mention that you find it strange that there's reinforced security everywhere, making it nearly impossible to enter certain cities, and you ask the reason why. However, Oreth seems quite uninformed about this — or perhaps he doesn't want to share what he actually knows.

He vaguely mentions that there have been several major thefts in the surrounding cities, and the guard is trying to track down the thieves, but there's no news yet on where they might be hiding. He speaks briefly about it, and you feel it's pointless to press him further — he's unlikely to share anything useful.

You can only speculate why.

Suddenly, he warms up to the conversation and explains that many people try to find a boat through 📖**Whitpoint** to get out, but since the bridge spanning the gorge collapsed, the 📖**Whitpoint** guard can't leave the city for now. This complicates their efforts to deploy enough soldiers to the surrounding cities. He chuckles and adds that there's a small cave under the bridge in the gorge wall (12-7), which leads directly into the city's sewer system and ends at the barracks near the main gate. If the guards weren't so lazy, they could easily bring in a small garrison and thoroughly search the southern forests for the thieves.

You can ask him about Kiena, in case he knows something about her (#76).

You can inquire about the local wine (#357).

You can sit at an empty table and order something to eat or drink (#109).

You can ask for a room to rest temporarily (#18).

You can look around the tavern and check out the people drinking there (#395).

Or you can leave the tavern and head back to the main square (#348).

#201

You estimate that Knireek and his crew are growing impatient waiting for your return.

You approach the table where you sat together earlier, and as you near it, you see Knireek and two of his companions still there, drinking and eating peacefully. You overhear them sharing stories, and one has just ended, prompting loud laughter from all three.

As you get closer, they make room for you to sit among them. One of them pushes his plate toward you, inviting you to take some food. You pinch off a bite before saying anything. The freshly roasted, crispy fish melts warmly in your mouth — add **+2** ⚡ points to yourself.

Knireek looks at you questioningly without saying a word.

If you have 🛒**the purple gem** and want to give it to them (#382).

If you've changed your mind, you can simply stand up and walk out (#143).

#202

You draw the sword from its scabbard, its hilt gleaming with crimson gems that catch the torchlight, casting fiery glints across the weathered wooden platform. You present it to the gathered crowd, their eyes widening at the vibrant scarlet stones nestled in intricate silver filigree. A hushed silence blankets the group, the air thick with anticipation, before their excited chatter erupts, voices buzzing about a potential challenger for the coveted ornate dagger, its blade shimmering with emerald and sapphire inlays.

The group leans in, scrutinizing the sword under the flickering glow of lanterns. One of them, a grizzled trader with a glint in his eye, taps the crimson gems with the dagger's polished obsidian hilt. The light strike sends a sickening crack through the air, the gems fracturing into a mosaic of dull, glassy shards. He crows with smug satisfaction, declaring your sword worthless, its dazzling red adornments nothing but cheap colored glass. With a dismissive flick, he tosses the blade back onto the platform, where it lands with a clatter on the scarred, amber-hued planks, the scattered gem fragments glinting mockingly in the light.

You stare, stunned, as the vibrant colors of your prized weapon betray you. A flush of shame burns your cheeks — had you inspected the sword's vivid gems yourself, you might have spared yourself this public disgrace in the heart of the bustling market square.

It's certainly better to leave the bustling main square for now; there's no point in enduring the gloating stares. You need to decide quickly — head southwest toward the harbor (#96) or, circling around the platform, take a quieter street northeast (#387).

#203

The tavern is very busy now, much like the marketplace. Inside, it's not particularly spacious, with only four or five tables, but it doesn't seem like more would ever be needed.

You approach the counter, where the bartender smiles kindly. From the snippets of conversation you overhear, you gather that the bartender's name is Kokary.

You can buy a mug of beer here for **1**⊛, which immediately grants **+1**⚡.

You can ask Kokary about Kiena (#82).

You can ask Kokary about the unusually high bustle in the village (#268).

Or you can head back to the marketplace, leaving the tavern behind (#6).

#204

You lean closer to the woodcutter, the crackling fire casting a warm, amber glow across his weathered face, and confess that you owe Kiena a handful of gleaming gold coins, eager to clear the debt after hearing whispers of her recent struggles. Your words hang in the air, mingling with the scent of pine and smoke from the hearth.

The woodcutter throws back his head, his hearty laugh echoing through the rustic tavern. He declares that Kiena is far from needy, his eyes twinkling like polished emeralds. Just two days ago, he says, he spotted her in the southern forests, where the trees drip with jade-green moss and sunlight fractures into golden shards through the canopy. That's bandit territory, he adds with a sly grin, and he's certain Kiena uncovered their elusive hideout, where those rogues now lurk, their coffers brimming with stolen jewels and shimmering silks from their latest heists.

Curiosity sparks in your chest, and you press him about these bandits, the firelight dancing in your eyes. He shrugs, his rough hands gesturing toward the unseen woods beyond the tavern's leaded windows. He roams the forest daily, he says, but its labyrinth of towering oaks and tangled vines has kept the bandits' camp hidden from him. Their hideout, he murmurs, is notoriously hard to find, cloaked in the dense, emerald heart of the woods. Then, leaning in, his voice drops to a conspiratorial whisper, as if the shadows themselves might eavesdrop. He's heard a rumor, he confides, that a trail of delicate white flowers — petals glowing like moonlit pearls against the forest floor — leads the bold straight to the bandits' lair, a secret path woven through the vibrant, untamed wilderness.

You can ask them about the forests around the city (#184).

Or, if that doesn't interest you, you can talk to the bartender instead (#281).

If you'd like to leave the tavern and return to the main square, you can do that too (#348).

#205

The local legends are quite vague and don't seem to make much sense at first glance.

The book recommended by Pap is about the legends of the Duland Heirs, attempting to describe the moonlit mysteries of the surrounding hills in the SShe language.

The book is written in an archaic style, but the language is easy to read and, in a way, translates as follows:

A little fairy girl, Sonia Norys, lived in a small forest hut. Her adorable face, reddish curls, rounded features, and always frosty smile made her irresistible to many men who visited her with the firm intention of winning her heart, as she had unwittingly stolen theirs.

Sonia unwittingly stole the hearts of many men, including that of Duland, a downy-cheeked apprentice blacksmith. The boy did everything to win Sonia, showering her with gifts, but her heart remained icy toward Duland, and his heart slowly broke with sorrow until, on a stormy night, he took his own life, sailing out onto the raging sea, never to return.

Afterward, suitors came and went at Sonia's door, but she paid them no mind. It so happened that one day, a new visitor arrived ~ Kate Wu. Kate was a long-haired, smiling girl from Dispel who came to the forest to live there herself. Thus, she met Sonia on a beautiful day, greeting her warmly. Sonia was just beginning to brew a valuable potion and invited Kate to help gather the ingredients.

The two girls quickly became friends, often going into the forest together to laugh and collect herbs. Soon, they did almost everything together, even selling their potions at the city market. On every free day, they packed their little cart and visited the city together.

What Sonia didn't know, however, was that Kate hadn't visited her by chance that day; she came with clear feelings in her heart, intending to steal and conquer Sonia's heart, as no one had succeeded before. As Kate and Sonia's friendship grew closer, Sonia's heart gradually filled with warm feelings for Kate.

But one day, something unexpected happened. Sonia was in the forest alone that day, gathering ingredients for a special new brew. Kate stayed at the hut to finish and bottle their latest batch, preparing everything for the big festive market in the coming days.

When Sonia returned, however, she was met with an unexpected coldness from Kate.

Kate didn't just want to kill Sonia that day; she wanted Sonia to suffer and feel her heart break before dying, just as her own had broken when Duland died.

With a sharp knife and vengeance, Kate awaited Sonia that day. Their deadly dance was brutal ~ Kate, with gleaming eyes, slowly plunged the blade into Sonia's soft flesh, and as Sonia's weak tears rolled down her face, her heart shattered with disappointment... In the end, Kate, her hands stained with Sonia's blood, slit her own throat, shedding one final tear for Duland.

Legend has it that Sonia's spirit sometimes appears under the blue moonlight among the hills, shedding a tear for Kate. Anyone who sees her has their heart break with sorrow on the spot.

Your mind wanders around the story.

Would you like another book about local legends? (#173)

Would you like to read about 📖Dispel's history? (#38)

Would you like to read about the Citadel? (#114)

Or have you had enough of legends and prefer to leave the bookstore for now? (#77)

#206

With a glint of excitement in your eyes, you venture into the shimmering, turquoise pool that floods the ancient chamber, its surface dancing with refracted light from unseen crystal veins in the walls. Each cautious step sends ripples swirling, as if the water itself whispers secrets of forgotten eras. You weave toward the chamber's far corner, where a jagged obsidian pillar leans at a daring angle, half-submerged like the tusk of some slumbering beast. The water, cool and tingling with a faint mineral hum, swirls around your boots, never cresting past their rugged leather rims, though it tugs playfully at your heels as if urging you to dive deeper.

Your heart races as you scan for hidden wonders – a concealed passage, a sunken vault, or perhaps the glint of some long-lost relic beneath the surface. The chamber's uneven stone floor, slick with algae and worn by centuries, shifts subtly underfoot, hinting at the ruins' ancient settling. Yet, as you reach the shadowed corner, your torchlight reveals only smooth, unyielding stone, carved with faint, weathered runes that pulse faintly in the flickering glow. No secret caves or hidden troves lie beneath these waters – just the quiet majesty of a chamber that has stood defiant against time's relentless march.

There's not much else of interest; there are two exits from this chamber. A narrow corridor leads southeast from here (#277), and through an opening to the east, you can see another chamber that appears to contain some kind of altar, as far as you can make out while standing in the water (#365).

#207

Captain Rottora tells you that they are now sailing up the Shorough River all the way to 📖**Ugmarlyther**, carrying food and clothing, along with some crates of medicinal herbs destined directly for the local doctor by special order.

He explains that they could set off any minute, as they're just waiting for the last crates to be loaded; once they're aboard, they'll raise the anchor. He mentions he'd normally ask for gold for the journey, but he'd prefer it if you acted as a warrior to protect the ship during the trip. They've been attacked by bandits several times, and much of their cargo has unfortunately ended up in the wrong hands. He'd be glad to have someone on deck at all times, but since they're not transporting particularly valuable goods and the profit isn't high, he can't afford to have a soldier on board for every trip. However, if you agree to stand guard over the ship and its cargo, he'd be happy to take you up the river in exchange.

It's up to you to decide if you like the offer and feel adequately armed for such a journey. It's highly likely that if you sail with Captain Rottora, you won't return to 📖**Dispel**. So, if you feel ready for the trip and have no more business to attend to here, you can take your place on the ship to depart (#392).

Alternatively, you can talk to Captain Davismore beforehand (#283).

Or, if you're not ready to leave 📖**Dispel** yet, the fish market is just a short distance from here (#320), or you can head toward the city marketplace (#181).

#208

You see a single guard running toward you. You'd like to catch your breath, but the path ahead still isn't clear.

Guard (with Sword)   11 ⚡6🗡 ⊙8→|←7🛡

Once you've dispatched the guard, you'll likely realize that word has already spread throughout the city about the fight at the western gate (#312).

#209

With a spark of daring in your chest, you stride through the raucous tavern, its air thick with the tang of spiced ale and the hum of whispered plots. Your eyes lock onto a trio huddled at a scarred oak table beneath a rack of gnarled antlers, their cloaks dusted with the salt of distant seas. You flash them a sly, knowing grin, as if you've unraveled their clandestine scheme. Their gazes snap to you — sharp, wary, like hawks sizing up a prowling fox — trying to parse whether you're a drunken fool or a blade seeking trouble.

Emboldened, you lean in, your voice a low, theatrical boom over the tavern's din. "I know exactly what you're plotting for the Citadel," you declare, chest puffed with bravado. "And I'm in — your cause needs a talent like mine!" The words hang in the smoky air, charged with challenge. The trio exchanges glances, their faces a mix of confusion and guarded amusement, clearly baffled by your cryptic accusation.

One of them, a weathered figure with a scar curling like a crescent moon across his cheek, rises slowly, his chair scraping against the rough-hewn floor. "Mate," he says, voice steady but edged with pity, "you've had one too many tankards. We're just fishers, docked for the night, setting sail at dawn's first light." His companions nod, stifling chuckles, their calloused hands cradling mugs of frothy ale.

A flush of realization hits you like a rogue wave — Bukatiz's nod toward the antlers must've pointed to another table, or his conspirators slipped into the night while you were distracted, weaving through the tavern's chaos. You stammer a quick apology, blaming the heady mulled wine for your blunder. "My mistake," you say with a sheepish grin, raising your hands in mock surrender. "Carry on, friends — may the tides favor your nets!" You pivot sharply, heart still racing with the thrill of your misstep, scanning the shadowed corners for the true plotters you were meant to find.

You can go back to the bartender (#270), or if you feel like sitting down now, you can join someone at another table who's peacefully sipping from their mug (#337).

#210

The room indeed overlooks the main square; from here, you can comfortably observe the bustling activity of the city's main square.

Since you came to rest, you lie down on the nomadic bed, which is much more uncomfortable than it first appears, as if you had to sleep on uneven ground filled with bumpy small and large stones. You don't find it comfortable at all, so after some tossing and turning, you give up the attempt.

You decide that you can rest later, especially once you've found Kiena.

Instead, you walk back down the stairs to the ground floor and throw yourself into the noisy bustle of the tavern (#5).

#211

Every nerve in your body is taut; you hold your breath as you watch the bushes, then you see a small wild boar family emerge. Two well-built adult specimens and five smaller, piglet-sized ones.

They also halt when they spot you in the middle of the path, and you stare at each other for a few long seconds. Then you make a sudden scaring motion, hoping it will frighten them and make them flee. On another day, your idea might work — the piglets do get a bit scared — but the parents are clearly going to protect their young from you.

You will need to protect yourself.

Wild Boar #1	12 ⚡ 💧 9 →|← 1 🛡
Wild Boar #2	14 ⚡ 💧 10 →|← 0 🛡

If you managed to defeat the wild boars (#73).

#212

You sit down next to one of the hobos, who has completely knocked himself out.

If this is the first time you're sitting next to him (#127), or if you've sat here before (#319).

#213

The trampled flowers' tracks quickly disappear before your eyes as the forest undergrowth thickens. After a while, you completely lose the tracks. You see a bunch of white flowers to your left, and some freshly cut logs in the right direction.

You can go left from here (#384), forward (#338), or even to the right (#92).

If you think you don't want to wander in the forest after all, you can still turn back from here (#50).

#214

With a surge of exhilaration, you ascend the ancient spiral staircase, its weathered stone steps twisting upward like the spine of a colossal dragon, each footfall echoing through the hollow tower as if awakening long-slumbering echoes. The air grows crisp and charged with the scent of wild winds as you emerge at the pinnacle, a lofty aerie perched atop the world, where the horizon stretches into infinity under a canopy of swirling, storm-tinged clouds.

From this vertiginous height, the landscape unfurls like a living tapestry woven by gods: to the south, jagged mountains pierce the sky, their snow-capped peaks gleaming under the sun's fierce gaze, while a serpentine river of molten silver bursts forth from their shadowed valleys, carving a path of glittering fury through the earth. Northward, rolling hills rise and fall in emerald waves, pierced by clusters of distant huts that huddle like forgotten sentinels, their thatched roofs catching fleeting rays of light amidst encroaching mists. To the east, an endless sea of primordial forest sprawls, a verdant labyrinth of towering ancients whose leaves whisper ancient curses, swallowing all light in their impenetrable depths.

Below, in the village's labyrinthine sprawl, shadowy figures dart like phantoms between crooked houses, their movements a silent ballet of intrigue and desperation, while the farther reaches lie eerily still, as if the settlement itself holds its breath against some unseen doom. The panorama is nothing short of awe-inspiring — a symphony of nature's raw power and mystery that steals your breath and ignites your spirit.

Yet, as you pivot to descend, a chilling, bone-dry rattle shatters the reverie, like the clatter of death's own dice. You whirl around, heart thundering, to behold a grotesque apparition clawing its way up the stairs: an animated skeleton, its hollow eye sockets blazing with unholy crimson fire, skeletal fingers gripping a rusted sword that gleams with malevolent intent, its jagged bones scraping against stone as it advances with relentless, otherworldly hunger.

Skeleton (with Sword)	6 ⚡1 ∿ ⊙6→|←1🛡

If you defeated the skeleton, there's really nothing more for you up here — it's time to head back down the spiral staircase to the tower's entrance hall (#329).

#215

You estimate that Knireek and his gang are growing impatient waiting for your return.

You approach the table where you sat together earlier, but as you near it, you don't see Knireek or his companions anywhere; others are peacefully drinking and eating there now.

It seems they didn't wait for you, or perhaps they have already left.

You pause for a moment and decide to go outside the tavern to look around (#143).

#216

The tavern is quite quiet now; the bartender loudly greets you and asks how he can serve you.

You can buy a mug of the local beer for **2**⊛; if you do, add **+1**⚡ point to yourself — the refreshing beer takes effect quickly.

You can ask the bartender if he's heard of Kiena (#57).

You can ask about the event in the main square (#259).

You can also leave the tavern and dive into the bustle of the main square (#107).

#217

You head toward the hand tool shop.

If this is your first time here (#98), or if you've been here before (#397).

#218

You crawl to the wall and lean against it, panting. This adventure with the thorn is hardly the highlight of your day. You look at your thigh and wonder if you made the right decision and when it will fully heal.

After a short rest and catching your breath, you decide it's time to continue the search. You didn't come here to be buried in a dirty underground cave system. Whatever fate brings, your primary goal is to find Kiena — and your secondary goal is to find the purple gem in these dungeons.

If you're still in an adventurous mood, you can examine the small pile of debris in the middle of the room (#108).

Or you can head north back into the tunnel (#234).

Alternatively, you can pass through the arched opening to the other similar room (#183).

#219

You're still close to the marketplace, just a few streets west from the main road, and in the bustle, you immediately find the way there — it's almost impossible to miss.

Here, you can practically buy and sell almost anything.

If you have a 🧺jar of honey, you can try to sell it here for **4**⊛.

If you have a 🧺flask of wine, you can try to sell it here for **7**⊛.

If you have a 🧺shovel, you can try to sell it here for **5**⊛.

If you have a 🧺flask of holy water, you can try to sell it here for **4**⊛.

You can buy a 🧺bouquet of yellow flowers (5-42) here for **1**⊛.

You can buy a 🧺👢pair of combat boots here for **9**⊛, which grants **+3**🏃 points.

You can buy a 🧺bundle of wheat here for **8**⊛.

You can buy a 🧺vial of elixir here for **7**⊛, which, when consumed once, grants **+12**⚡.

If you no longer want to linger at the market, you can head toward the tavern (#340).

You can cut through a few smaller streets, cross the main road, and head northeast toward the wheat fields (#164).

Or you can head northwest behind the houses and return to the main road leading out of the village (#118).

Alternatively, you can leave the city south through the forests (#347).

#220

You spot the smoke rising from the blacksmith's chimney from afar, the master is surely working hard right now. The workshop and hut stand alone at this crossroads; Bukatiz must be envious of it, as you couldn't find a better or more convenient location for travelers passing through even if you tried.

Youngrek waves from a distance as he sees you approaching, clearly having a friendly warm heart despite his rugged appearance, and it may well be that he literally forges gold from this warmth in the end.

At the junction, a signpost points toward two villages in opposite directions.

You can continue your journey toward 📖**Moonward** from here, boldly following the road and leaving 📖**Dispel** behind, in the southwest direction (#363).

You can continue your journey toward 📖**Oceastall** from here, northwest (#99).

Naturally, you can go back from here along the path behind the houses toward the harbor and fish market (#320).

You can walk up alongside the city walls to the Wamake Gate (#140).

Or you can visit Youngrek's workshop (#385).

#221

You examine the crests; you've seen similar ones on the T'lindilhei battlefield, but here the crests are in much better condition than on the armor of the battlefield victims or the rotting flags there.

The crest itself doesn't depict any single animal, and clearly no weapons can be made out on it either. Rather, its main motif is some kind of mystical orb shape surrounded by lightning. All of this on a completely blue background. They mean absolutely nothing to you; obviously, they try to symbolize some kind of magic or something related to magic.

Beyond that, there's nothing else interesting about them; three crests each are carved and painted on the stone walls, symmetrically on all four walls, facing each other. The only interesting thing that only becomes apparent after longer staring is that the arrangement and shape of the crests on opposite walls are exactly the mirror image of those on the facing wall. This certainly has significance too, perhaps some magical effect around the coffin, because the coffin is positioned exactly at the center of the four sets of three symbols, which is surely no accidental coincidence.

If you're curious after this and haven't opened the coffin yet, you can try it (#267), or you can leave this small room and head back to the corridor (#45).

#222

A well-trodden small path leads to the farm, and as you get closer, you hear a strange deep-toned buzzing sound more and more strongly, which has been in your ears for a while. You think you see small dark clouds swirling around the little boxes near the house, which you view suspiciously, then suddenly it all comes together: this is a beekeeper's farm, the little boxes standing on legs around the house are beehives, and the buzzing sound is the monotonous roar of the industrious bees.

It's quite scary, and as you look, the path to the house indeed requires cutting through the beehives — and the wildly swirling swarms.

You can risk the path to the house (#135).

You can turn back on the road; from here, you can still do so safely (#31).

#223

With a knot tightening in your gut, you weave through the dimly lit tavern, shadows flickering like watchful eyes from the hearth's dying embers. The air hangs heavy with the scent of stale ale and unspoken secrets, and you can feel the weight of curious stares from nearby patrons as you approach the trio at their scarred table, cloaked in hooded murmurs. You fix them with a knowing glance as you imply you've pierced their veil of conspiracy.

Their eyes narrow in unison, a mix of intrigue and menace, as they appraise you like a thief eyeing a mark. One shifts subtly, his hand drifting toward the hilt of a concealed dagger, while another scans the room for eavesdroppers, his jaw set in quiet alarm. Are you a harmless sot, or a spy sent to unravel them? The tension coils like a spring, the tavern's rowdy clamor fading into a distant hum.

Emboldened by desperation, you lean in close, your voice a hushed boast laced with feigned confidence: "I know precisely what you're scheming at the Citadel, and I want in — my skills could tip the scales for your... endeavor." The words escape like a dare, hanging in the smoky air, and for a heartbeat, you wonder if you've just signed your own warrant.

They exchange furtive looks, the silence stretching taut as a bowstring, before one gestures discreetly — almost reluctantly — for you to join them, his eyes never leaving yours. You slide into the seat, every creak of the wood amplifying the unease, aware that a wrong word could spark violence in this den of rogues.

"What exactly do you think you know?" the scarred leader murmurs, his tone low and probing, fingers drumming an impatient rhythm on the table. You swallow hard, recounting the rumors you've gleaned about the Citadel's hidden vaults brimming with forbidden treasures, your words tumbling out in a rush. You confess your dire need for gold — the locals' wariness has dried up honest work, forcing you toward riskier paths — but you can't afford to rot in Dispel forever. You stop speaking but you know that you'll slip away soon, destination unknown, driven by the urgent hunt for Kiena.

The three-person group listens with enjoyment to what you share, and they're not stingy with you. Despite having just pickpocketed a drunk, they buy you a glass of fine local wine, which gives you **+3⚡**, just during the conversation.

Then one of them, who calls himself Knireek — likely the gang leader — takes over and explains that they're not just interested in the Citadel's treasures but are seeking a special purple gem that — presumably — has some kind of magical effect. He doesn't say it outright, but he strongly hints at it, making it quite valuable to them.

You ponder that such a gem could be useful to you too...

If you want to make yourself seem valuable, you can try to convince them that you know everything about the Citadel's structure and that you're the right person for the job (#265).

If this heist seems too big a bite, you can leave them and head to the tavern counter (#195).

Or you can even walk straight out of the tavern (#143).

#224

You stand in a significantly smaller room, with a beautiful altar positioned on the far wall.

> The mud reaches up to your knees, making it quite difficult and unsteady to proceed. You stumble and trip, it's a wonder you can keep your balance. Roll two dice, and if the resulting number is greater than your � points, deduct **-1⚡** from yourself as you trip in the mud, fall, and suffer a minor injury.

On the altar lie a few freshly cut bluish flowers.

On the room's left-hand wall, opposite the altar, you see a grated opening. As far as you can tell, it might be the same room where you climbed down the ladder to get here; you can see the locals busily working there.

> If you have 💡**a bouquet of yellow flowers**, you can try placing it on the altar by adding the two numbers together, subtracting from this chapter's number, and continuing there.

There's only one way out of the room, back to the chamber you came from (#308).

You can try taking the blue flower from the altar (#345).

#225

As you travel along the road, a suffocating feeling increasingly takes hold of you, as if you're not alone, but you can't precisely define the feeling or its origin. The wide stone road itself is no different from what you've seen or experienced so far, with nothing interesting visible nearby or in the distance, so this otherworldly feeling doesn't fit the picture at all.

Of course, you can continue your journey north along the wide road (#343).

Or you can keep going south on the road (#91).

#226

You slide the shimmering vial onto the weathered oak table, its iridescent liquid swirling like captured starlight under the flickering torchlight. Knireek's piercing gaze locks onto it, his brow furrowing in deep suspicion, as if the tiny vessel harbors a storm ready to unleash chaos.

You lean forward, voice laced with urgency, explaining how this elixir hones the senses to razor-sharp precision — heightening reflexes, amplifying every whisper of wind and glint of steel — making him an unstoppable force in the heat of battle, dodging strikes that would fell lesser warriors.

He pauses, his massive frame tensing like a coiled serpent, eyes distant as shadows of memory dance across his scarred face. Then, in a gravelly rumble that cuts through the tavern's din, he launches into a harrowing tale: of his fierce brother, a legendary blade-master, who once cornered a vengeful witch in a moonlit glen. Instead of delivering the fatal blow, he spared her twisted life, only for her to cackle and press a glowing phial into his calloused palm. "Drink this," she hissed, her voice like cracking ice, "and no foe shall ever claim victory over you again."

The brother, emboldened by the promise of godlike prowess, clutched the potion like a talisman of destiny. But when the clash of war drums echoed and he uncorked it in the frenzy of combat — gulping it down amid clashing swords and war cries — agony exploded through him like wildfire in his veins. He collapsed in a writhing heap, foam flecking his lips, his screams echoing across the blood-soaked field as the poison ravaged his body from within. And in that cruel twist, the witch's prophecy rang true: dead before the battle's end, he never faced another opponent who could defeat him.

Knireek's lips curl into a wry, battle-hardened smirk as he shoves the vial back toward you with a deliberate, unyielding push, his voice dropping to a low growl. "Aye, potions like this do exactly what you say... but I'll wager this one's got its own deadly punchline. Save it for your own desperate hour, friend — test its fire on your skin, not mine."

The air crackles with unspoken challenge, leaving you gripping the vial tighter, heart pounding at the edge of temptation and peril.

If you have anything else from the following that you can offer him, now's the time to put it on the table.

If you have 🧺**a large basket of fish** and leave it as collateral (#25).

If you have 🧺**a hooded cloak** and leave it as collateral (#323).

If you have 🧺**a leather glove** and leave it as collateral (#79).

If you don't have any of these, or simply don't trust them enough to leave anything behind, you can simply stand up and walk back to the tavern counter (#195).

#227

You take the sword in hand and slide the blade between the door panel and the wall; it seems the door will give way, and when you hear a painful metallic crack, you smile.

> However, your joy is short-lived, because instead of the hinge rivets, a small piece breaks off from your sword's blade. You look disappointedly at the wrought iron steel — this isn't a good sign. This means **-2 →|←** points from your sword's current damage value.

Somewhat disappointed, you can leave the kitchen by crawling back through the small opening toward the corridor from where you originally came (#191).

Or if you still feel adventurous, you can take a closer look at the stacked shelves on the opposite wall (#333).

#228

You knock, and after a short wait, the oak door slowly opens. An older man looks at you questioningly. You ask if you saw correctly that a healer lives here, to which the old man nods and asks back if there's anything he can help you with.

You can tell him you'd like to speak with the healer (#66).

Or politely say goodbye and continue on your way (#322).

#229

You drift through the bustling heart of the city, aimlessly looking around, where sunlight glints off cobblestone streets lined with honey-hued stone buildings. 📖**Dispel's** inner, central part isn't really for visitors — mostly the middle class and the wealthier reside within the protective walls, their homes adorned with splashes of crimson banners and verdant window boxes.

It's a friendly little city, though in a few darker corners, shrouded in indigo shadows, one or two beggars appear. You try to avoid them — you don't have much yourself, and right now, you're certainly not able to help them. You stroll a few streets among the alcoves, trying to catch snippets of conversations, but you can't quite connect the everyday problems of the locals here, their voices mingling with the faint aroma of spiced bread wafting from nearby stalls.

> As you amble along, a strange feeling comes over you, and your suspicion wasn't unfounded — someone unnoticed unhooked one of your small purses from your belt while you were distracted. This carelessness cost you **-3**⚙, deduct it from yourself.

A surge of fury boils up inside you as you whirl around, eyes darting wildly through the teeming crowd, every shadowed alley and fleeting face a potential suspect. Your pulse hammers in your ears, the air thick with the clamor of voices and footsteps that could mask an escape — or worse, an ambush. But the theft feels like a ghost from longer than moments ago, the cunning pilferer already swallowed by the chaotic throng, leaving you exposed and seething.

Gritting your teeth in bitter defeat, you forced yourself to accept the irreplaceable loss, feeling a knot of unease tightening in your gut.

From where you stand, you have a good view of the stairs leading up to the Citadel — you can check that out more closely (#41). You can also visit the tavern in the central square (#113) if you like, or if you've had enough of the local bustle, you can walk out through the main gate and leave the inner city district (#149).

#230

With a cheerful grin and a dramatic flourish of his hand, Jarse waves you on like a proud chef urging a guest to savor the last bite. "Go ahead, polish off that meal – can't have you adventuring on an empty stomach!" he chuckles warmly. Between hearty chomps, you casually ask how on earth to wield this quirky potion later on.

"Ah, my friend, it's basically the world's sneakiest essential oil," he replies with a wink, leaning in like he's sharing a hilarious family secret. "Pops anyone carrying a weapon right into dreamland. Just twist off that cap and – poof! – magic does its goofy dance."

He pauses mid-gesture, his eyes widening comically as he switches to a mock-serious tone, pointing at you with exaggerated concern. "But hey, buddy, do me a favor: scoot those weapons of yours a smidge farther away when you pop it open. Otherwise, you'll be the one snoring like a hibernating bear in two shakes!" He bursts into a hearty laugh, slapping his knee. "Trust me, that's not the heroic nap you want in the middle of a scrap – waking up to find the bad guys tying bows on your boots!"

You chuckle along and quickly shuffle your gear aside, not wanting to be the punchline. Jarse, still grinning ear-to-ear, gives a playful nod of approval before cracking the vial's cap just a teensy bit. Out wafts this whimsical bluish-purple vapor, twirling like a tipsy fairy around your weapons in a fluffy little cloud, putting on a short-lived show before vanishing without a whiff or whisper.

"See? Whoever that cheeky cloud sniffs out with a blade or bow zonks out for a quick siesta," he explains with a friendly pat on your back. "Then they bounce right back after a short while, fresh as a daisy – no headaches, no regrets. Just don't blame me if you end up using it on a squirrel with a pointy acorn!" laughs hard at his joke.

He pushes the 🛒**vial with the essential oil (4-17)** toward you meaningfully; since you've already paid for it, you probably don't need to ponder much whether to take it with you.

You finish eating; his kindness felt good, add **+5⚡** points to yourself. You chat a bit more, then wave goodbye to him, and ponder which road to continue your journey on from here. To the north, you see a bridge; you can go that way (#39), or to the east, you can follow the city wall among the houses (#238).

#231

You estimate that Knireek and his gang are already impatiently waiting for you to return.

You walk to the table where you sat together earlier, but as you approach, you don't see Knireek or his companions anywhere; others are peacefully drinking and eating there now.

It seems they didn't wait for you after all, or perhaps they have already left.

You ponder for a moment and decide to go outside the tavern to look around (#143).

#232

Amid the warm glow of lantern light casting golden hues across the tavern's wooden beams, you find yourself welcomed by a ragtag bunch — not the fairest faces in the realm, with their mismatched beards and weathered grins, but their rosy cheeks flushed from merry mugs of ale make them all the more inviting. They've clearly embraced the lively cheer, pulling out a stool for you with boisterous laughs and claps on the back, as if you've been old pals for ages.

Beneath their hearty exteriors — cloaked in earthy browns and faded greens — they bubble with good-natured chatter, sharing tales that dance like fireflies in the air. You can't quite pin down if they're wandering dreamers chasing legends or steadfast locals watching over the hearth, but one thing's crystal clear: they know every nook of this cozy tavern, from the sweetest honeyed mead to the friendliest customs that keep the gathering alive with harmless fun.

> If you have ♀**a bottle of local wine**, you can use it here by multiplying the two numbers and subtracting that from this chapter's number, then continue reading there.

You can ask them about Kiena (#95).

If you have **6**⊛, you can buy the group a bottle of wine and try to extract information from them (#349).

Or you can leave them and talk to the bartender instead (#281).

#233

However you look at it, you don't want to seem aggressive — the sparks of fear glittered in those eyes — so you walk through the swarms of bees to a safe distance. You're not sure if the bees were less aggressive on the way back or if you just didn't notice them, but it feels like you got far fewer stings. This only costs you **-1⚡** point now.

At a safe distance from the beehives but still on the farm, you actually lie down for a bit to gather new strength for the rest of your journey. You're just about to head off when you see the house door open, and a young woman — or perhaps a girl — steps out. She walks among the beehives, and you can clearly see the swirling bees avoiding her, giving her free passage wherever she goes. You've heard of spells that can control animals, but you've never seen anything like it with your own eyes until this very moment, if it's even magic at work.

You finally stand up and watch the bees' elegant dance around the girl for a few moments.

If you feel like it and still have the energy, you can try talking to her again (#128).

Or you can finally leave the farm behind if you'd like (#31).

#234

You barely take four or five steps before you run into a T-shaped junction.

The longer branch of the tunnel leads south (#295).

You can go north from here (#163).

You can go southwest from here along a corridor occasionally lined with stones (#326).

#235

You've already taken down the only map you found useful; the empty spot is still on the wall. The other maps don't seem particularly interesting, and you're still unsure which cities or more precisely which parts of them some maps depict.

If you'd like, you can examine the books before leaving (#350).

There's one exit from here: this door leads back to the smoking room (#386).

#236

You nod friendly to the owner, and you already have a few topics in mind that you'd like to read more about, but in this chaos, it's impossible to find anything on your own without Pap's assistance.

Would you like to read about 📖 **Dispel's** history (#38)?

Would you like to read about the Citadel (#114)?

Would you like to read about the surrounding legends (#205)?

Or have you had enough of reading for now, and would you rather look for something more exciting outside (#77)?

#237

You wander through the dense forest, spotting white flowers to your left.

You can go left from here (#134), or even forward (#78).

#238

You walk along the path beside the city wall, passing a few crumbling little houses, but after one turn, you find a quite neat small open blacksmith workshop, from whose chimney a gray smoke column curls upward in a friendly manner.

If this is your first time here (#304), or if you've been here before (#16).

#239

The short tunnel ends in a smaller chamber. In the center of the room, there is a statue depicting a person; the sculptor captured some kind of sailor motif or moment in the clothing and posture, but the figure's attire isn't particularly tied to the sea or sailing, at least not to modern eyes.

It might be worth examining the statue more closely (#129).

The room has two exits: one leads south (#23), the other east, continuing in a narrow tunnel where you can only proceed by crawling (#89).

#240

As you continue along the road, a small village comes into view as you descend from one of the hills. It seems there's not much life in the village, at least from afar; you don't see any people, and perhaps only a single column of smoke appears in the distance — but even that seems to come from outside the village, from the farther side.

It looks quite ominous that everything is so deserted, but your curiosity is stronger nonetheless.

You slowly enter between the houses, and what you saw from afar is even more true up close — the village is almost empty, with only a few worried, scrutinizing eyes following you as you proceed.

You decide to go straight to the tavern and try to find out what happened here (#199).

#241

With a gentle tremor in your hands, born from the day's weary travels, you draw out the bouquet of vibrant blue flowers and extend them toward Freela, the heart and soul of this cozy tavern she's tended for years.

"Oh, beautiful flowers, stranger!" Freela's eyes light up with a soft, genuine warmth, a flicker of unexpected joy softening the lines of fatigue etched around them from long nights pouring ale and listening to woes.

She accepts the blooms with a tender grasp, her fingers brushing yours briefly, before nestling them into a half-full mug of frothy beer like a cherished keepsake. You pause, brow furrowed in quiet confusion, but she sets the impromptu vase on the counter with such effortless grace, as if it's the most natural tribute in her world — a small act that stirs a pang of curiosity in your chest.

"I'll tell you a secret, stranger," she murmurs, leaning in closer, her voice dropping to a conspiratorial whisper laced with a hint of vulnerability. "Blue is my favorite color." It rings true, and as your gaze sweeps the tavern — her tavern, alive with azure curtains billowing like gentle waves, delicate ribbons fluttering in sapphire shades, faded dried blooms pinned to the walls like memories preserved — now joined by this fresh bouquet in its humble mug, a quiet ache tugs at you; perhaps it's more than a color, a thread woven into her very spirit.

"Is that the big secret?" you inquire, your tone laced with a weary amusement, as you absentmindedly rest your weapon on the counter, the clink echoing a touch too loudly in the intimate space. Freela flinches back ever so slightly, a shadow of old pain crossing her features, before she appraises you anew — your road-worn form, the scarred hilt of your blade — her eyes searching yours with a mix of caution and unspoken sorrow, as if gauging whether you're friend or another fleeting storm. "Can't handle sharp weapons?" you tease lightly, hoping to lighten the air.

"I hate them," Freela replies, her voice cracking just a fraction with raw emotion, urging you to whisk the offending items away from her sight. "And I hate the patrolling guards who arbitrarily block your way. Just like on the road leading north..."

She tells you she has a friend in 🗺 **Moonward**, Jarse, whom she can only visit by going through the forest, far avoiding the stone road, at the moment. If you do her a favor and bring her a potion from Jarse, she'll treat you to a mug of beer — no need to pay for it. Just tell Jarse that Freela sent you (23-6).

You slowly sip the cool brew, and it's time to figure out your next step.

If you'd like to order another mug of the local beer, it will still cost **2**✸ if you have the money for such indulgence (#150).

If you think it's time to leave the tavern, you can do that too (#394).

#242

You begin the storytelling, recounting everything from the beginning about how the dungeon and chamber system beneath the Citadel was built over time, part of which was later converted into the sewer system. During the constructions, they weren't entirely careful everywhere, and at certain points, the sewer system isn't sealed off from the dungeons; in many places underground, the two tunnel systems are passable without any obstacles.

The only thing you don't know is where in the city you can find an entrance to the sewer system that's out of sight and won't be noticed by the guards.

Knireek says they've been in the city for weeks and know every nook and cranny. They also know you can somehow get from the sewers to the Citadel, but they have no map of it. It could take them days to find such a passage. However, they know the inner city is heavily guarded by soldiers, but outside the city wall — especially around the wretched little tents and huts by the riverbank — they hardly patrol at all.

There's a secluded entrance to the sewer system there, which they've already scouted out to go underground, and it might be perfect for you to start through and find the entrance or passage to the Citadel's chamber system.

Knireek takes out a key, which he claims he stole from one of the guards a few days ago. He says you can use it to open the sewer system's locks. You take the key; it's nothing more than a 🧺 **rusty iron key**, into which two digits have been scratched: **7-3**.

You carefully put it away.

Knireek says they'll stay in the tavern and wait for you until you return.

You nod approvingly, stand up from the table, and head toward the tavern exit (#143).

#243

You continue running down the main street, bumping into a small group who slow you down a bit as you dash through them.

The guards are hot on your heels.

You can continue along the main road from here (#372), or turn left into a small street (#369).

#244

You confidently walk along the wide stone road, with a few travelers passing by, some pulling small horse-drawn carts, but everyone is peacefully making their way.

You stop for a moment to catch your breath.

You can continue north from here (#12).

You can continue south from here (#123).

#245

The grated gate stands imposingly before you, its thick iron bars forged into an unyielding lattice that's embedded deep into the ancient stone walls of the Citadel, far more robust and intimidating than the flimsy grilles you've pried open in forgotten ruins past — each bar as thick as your toe, cold to the touch and humming with the faint echo of distant drafts. It swings outward on heavy hinges that gleam with fresh oil, the lock a polished brass mechanism designed solely for entry from the outside, its keyhole winking mockingly in the dim torchlight as if guarding secrets meant only for the initiated. This chamber, with its faint scent of polished metal and lingering incense, clearly serves as a well-trodden hub within the fortress; the gate's pristine condition speaks of regular passage — hinges silent and smooth, the lock free of even a speck of rust, suggesting watchful guardians or frequent visitors who maintain it with meticulous care.

Peering through the bars, you catch the shadowy contours of a narrow staircase spiraling upward into obscurity, its worn steps curving like the coils of a serpent ascending toward unseen heights, flecked with motes of dust dancing in stray beams of light. Yet, frustration builds as your fingers grip the unbudging iron, the tantalizing path beyond remaining just out of reach — if you can't breach this formidable barrier, the mysteries it conceals might as well be entombed forever in the Citadel's depths.

You grab the grates, give them a little shake, but there's no chance of opening the gate without a key.

However, you can examine the small chest in the corner (#309).

You can start exploring the side corridor (#152).

Or you can crawl back through the narrow and damp tunnel you came from (#33).

#246

You can't run further on this road; you're forced to turn back from where the guards are already hot on your heels. You can't avoid facing them if you want to continue your path toward the harbor.

Guard #1 (with Sword)	10⚡5🗡 ⊙5→|←5🛡
Guard #2 (with Sword)	11⚡4🗡 ⊙4→|←9🛡
Guard #3 (with Sword)	12⚡7🗡 ⊙7→|←8🛡

If you defeated the guards (#346).

#247

The statue still leans against the wall, and the spear remains motionless, pointing toward the sky as you left it last time. But no matter how much you examine the statue and its pedestal again in the hope that you might have missed something before, this time you find nothing new on it.

Two paths lead onward from the room.

You can go south from here (#23).

You can go east from here (#89).

#248

You take out the sword adorned with red gems and show it to them. A brief silence falls, then the chatter resumes as the small group on the platform eagerly announces that there might be a challenger for the ornate dagger.

They examine the sword more closely, and one of them strikes the gems with the harder side of the dagger, causing a piece to chip off from the dagger's hilt. He shouts loudly that the sword is a true masterpiece adorned with real gems, and he's willing to pay up to **10**✷ for it. It's up to you whether you accept the offer and want to sell the sword to them for that amount.

He puts away the dagger and takes out an ornate hourglass, exclaiming that they're now seeking a challenger for this precious item, and they're curious if anyone can show a more expensive or valuable relic.

> If you have a ♀**golden compass**, you can show it by multiplying the two numbers, adding the result to this chapter's number, and continuing your reading there.

If you feel like you can't or don't want to show them anything now, you can visit the tavern on the other side of the square (#216).

Or you can leave this bustle behind and head southwest toward the harbor (#96), or follow the narrower street behind the platform northeast (#387).

#249

"Everyone has heard a lot about her; there are too many strangers here" the guard barks, and it seems he has no intention of saying more or letting you go.

However, you can easily bypass them to enter the city (#59), or perhaps head back to the harbor (#1).

The marketplace (#181) is also just a few corners away, where you can surely buy food and clothing.

#250

The door opens silently, and you enter a library-like room. Two walls have floor-to-ceiling bookshelves, the third has a fireplace with a very comfortable-looking chair in front of it, and the fourth wall is adorned with various maps.

> You hear noises and voices from upstairs – you're not alone in the house! Roll two dice; if the result is greater than your ✍ points, unfortunately you failed to stay silent and unnoticed – continue the story here (#13).

If you'd like to examine the books (#350).

If you'd like to examine the maps hanging on the wall (#61).

The only exit from here leads back to the smoking room (#386).

#251

As you approach the table, you see that most of the food has already rotted or become moldy.

There's not much to see here anymore.

If you wish, you can head northeast through a small opening to another chamber (#263), or you can continue through a corridor in the far wall leading northwest (#191).

#252

As you start walking toward them, they immediately scatter, and by the time you reach the corner where they stood, they've already found a safe hiding place in one of the similarly abandoned houses or somewhere among them.

You shake your head, even though you really just wanted to talk to them — it seems they didn't want to talk to you.

If you've seen enough of the village, you can walk back the way you came (#116).

Or you can continue down the main street, hoping to find something far more interesting (#289).

#253

Interestingly, the books mention only one certain name as owner, and that is Gaki Chakgrek, the founder.

> **T**he people of Dysp'l leave this estate to Gaki, who, after his tormented fate, can live in rightful peace among his beloved people. Let these walls always be Gaki's, without questioning or doubt, we all bow in agreement and give this to him.

> "Forever yours this estate, Gaki, our adored leader, and as a sign of our homage, accept our eternal gift every year, the finest harvest, and the intoxicating drink from the pressing of the chole Gemoon chemn."

As far as you can make out from the continuation, after Gaki's death, the estate became a sanctuary, the stone walls and towers surrounding the sanctuary were built from the city's common respect and strength. Mostly holy people inhabited the place and cared for it over the years, but it had no real owner.

One of the books mentions the rebuilding after the fire, but it seems that it operated on a voluntary basis from the city's inhabitants – and with a little nudging from the soldiers.

> **T**he city of Dyspel unanimously sacrifices from its time and purse to avenge the damage of the sad fires, and to rebuild its eternal sanctuary in even greater splendor, showing the imperishability of time.

> This sacrifice requires every man, woman, and child, whose heritage is this place, to raise the memory of this immortal place to greatness again with their devout work.

It also emerges from the writing that at this time, many left the city because of the forced labor, and tried to settle elsewhere in hopes of honestly profitable work. Almost every writing mentions one place multiple times, a certain 📖**Ugmarlyther** named village – or city –

that grew out of the ground around this time, heading upstream along the river, not too far from here.

In its current form, the Citadel is guarded by a religious congregation called Duland's Heirs, and with quite careful and loving care — at least based on the descriptions.

> **S**onia Norys, who was the innocent child of nature, in memory we raise these walls to greatness and sacrifice in spirit for Sonia's last tears. Flowers and gardens, where Sonia's lost soul can always find home among us.
>
> We do not fear their hearts, Sonia's love shines on us, as her love shone once and only once.

If you wish, you can read more on other topics about the Citadel (#114), or simply stop reading and try further in the fresh air (#77).

#254

Wandering in the dense forest, you catch sight of a few freshly cut logs to your left.

You can go left from here (#32), or even right (#137).

#255

The medieval harvest celebration erupts with vibrant cheer under a canopy of garlands woven from golden wheat, bright gourds, and crimson leaves, strung festively between ancient oaks encircling the village green. Torches and lanterns cast a warm, twinkling glow, illuminating villagers in colorful tunics twirling to a merry band's tunes – a flute's lilting melodies, a fiddle's sprightly jigs, and a drum's lively beat sparking raucous laughter and spirited dances. Children, faces smeared with berry juice from pie-eating contests, flail in gleeful, rhythm-less abandon, while dogs, tails wagging like banners, bound joyfully among them, snatching dropped crumbs and chasing fluttering ribbons.

Tables groan with harvest bounty: crusty bread, herb-flecked cheeses, and pitchers of spiced cider steaming with cinnamon. Over a crackling bonfire, iron racks sizzle with venison and pork, the cook's booming cry of "Feast, all ye merry!" drawing eager crowds as he serves juicy portions amid tales of bountiful fields. Jugglers toss flaming torches, and singers belt bawdy ballads, amplifying the festive din.

You eye a grassy spot to bask in the joyous chaos, but calamity strikes: two massive hounds, lost in a playful chase, crash into the grilling racks, sending meats flying in a wild arc. The dogs freeze, then pounce on the scattered morsels with gleeful yips, joined by smaller curs in a frenzied feast. Flames flare, charring the rest to ash. The music halts, laughter fading to gasps as the celebration's high spirits crash into stunned dismay, the sudden loss of the feast casting a fleeting shadow over the vibrant moments.

If you have 🧺**a large basket of fish** with you, you might be able to sell it here on the spot with good business sense (#165).

If you don't have anything like that, or just don't want to sell it, then leaving the now awkward celebration, you can walk back between the houses to the marketplace from here (#6).

#256

You cautiously step toward the small coffin on the altar.

If this is the first time you are examining it (#40), if you have already examined the coffin before (#306).

#257

You rush down a narrow street, where you can see the city wall on your right.

The guards are hot on your heels.

You can go forward from here (#68), or turn left (#305).

#258

The skeleton collapses as you deliver the final blow, giving you a moment to look around, but there's nothing to see in the chamber. As you linger, the previously neutralized skeleton begins to stir again, as if begging for a rematch.

Skeleton (with Sword)	13 ⚡ 4 🗡 ⊙6 →|← 2 🛡

If you've put an end to the skeleton's stirring once more, it might now be truly safer to leave this room (#376).

#259

The bartender sighs, saying that these comedians arrived here a few days ago, or at least based on their boasting, they seem to be, trying to outdo everyone in everything, as far as their loudness today reveals, they display valuable items and challenge the townspeople to try to show them something even more interesting.

You don't need to think about it for more than a moment that the town is certainly dealing with well-organized thieves, but for now, you keep your opinion to yourself. You just say to the bartender, shrugging your shoulders, that maybe you'll check them out closer later, it seems like interesting entertainment.

You can ask the bartender if he's heard of Kiena (#57).

You can also go out to the main square's hustle and bustle (#107).

#260

Freela sits down next to you with a warm smile, sliding over a steaming mug of spiced beer that fills the air with hints of cinnamon and honey, her easy manner inviting you to lean in and chat like old friends. She starts talking about the local harvest, her voice bubbling with enthusiasm: "This year's bound to be a cracker — perfect weather's blessed us, and the ears are plump with grains. We've already hauled in loads from the surrounding fields, though the granary's the real headache; it's flooded again, so no storing the crop there just yet."

You look puzzled, glancing around the cozy space where soft blue lanterns cast a welcoming glow and patrons share laughter over frothy ales, since you haven't spotted any flooding in the village. Freela laughs heartily, her eyes twinkling as she refills your mug without asking. "Ah, don't fret — it's all tucked underground in a cool spot to keep those grains fresh as dawn till they hit the mill. Keeps 'em safe and sound."

You ask where the granary is, and she nods encouragingly, gesturing with her tankard. "Out at the edge of the northern wheat fields, love. If you're up for it, head over — the villagers are bucketing out the water now, and they'd welcome an extra pair of hands. It's our yearly ritual after winter, but we make it fun with songs and shared flasks. Long ago, we even set up an altar down there to the god of abundance, but — ha! — seems they've showered us with water alongside the bounty!"

You inquire about the altar, and Freela's face lights up, drawing you deeper into the tale with a conspiratorial wink. "My ancestors built it ages back, a fine stone tribute in those depths. Come harvest eve, we carry down a basket overflowing with vibrant blooms as thanks. The gods must approve, for they tint every petal in the radiant blue of our deity of plenty — join us sometime; it's a sight that warms the soul, just like this beer."

Freela leans back against the bar with a contented grin, her fingers dancing along the rim of her tankard as the soft blue lanterns above cast a warm, inviting glow, their light shimmering like a twilight sky across the cozy tavern. She picks up the thread of her tale with a proud, merchant's gleam in her eye: "And well, the crop, as every year, is bountiful — enough to brim our stores and beyond. We often keep 📖**Moonward** and 📖**Whitpoint** fed through winter's bite, and they're mighty grateful, sending back their thanks in shining gold, naturally. Won't be any different this year; just need to dry out that granary, same old song and dance."

Freela is in a good mood, and she puts down **+1**⊛ in front of you so that if you want to drink another beer of hers, she'll cover half of it now. If you feel like adding another **1**⊛ from your pouch and drinking another one, there's nothing stopping you (#150).

If you've seen enough of the tavern, you can leave it (#394).

#261

You are in the southern cell, faint lights filter in from above through a very narrow ventilation opening, barely wider than your fist, obviously not ideal for any escape plans. However, a slight breath of fresh air comes through it, which, strangely enough, you find particularly refreshing right now.

In the cell, a pile of rotten hay lies in the corner; if you have the stomach for it, you can search through it (#339).

In the corner, you see a small wooden chest; it might be worth examining it (#85).

If you think you've seen enough here, you can leave the cell (#280).

#262

You take out the flask filled with wine and offer it to him.

"Ah, the wine!" he takes it from you and tastes it. "What do you want in exchange for this, my friend?"

You can ask for gold in return (#336).

You can ask about Kiena (#80).

You can ask who he is (#373).

You can ask about the weapons (#381).

If you think this situation is already surreal enough, you can even go back through the forest to the main road (#50).

#263

You stand at the bottom of a spiral staircase in a small circular chamber. The staircase obviously leads up to the tower's ground-floor room, while to the northeast and northwest you see massive closed doors, and you can't tell what they might conceal; however, to the southwest, you can walk through a smaller opening into another chamber.

You can go northwest through the oak door (#180).

You can go northeast by opening the iron-bound door (#368).

You can walk through the southwest opening to the other chamber (#396).

Or you can go up the spiral staircase (#329).

#264

As unbelievable as it may seem, there is no way forward from here, and you can't escape further from the angered guards by zigzagging through the streets. To get to the harbor, you must cut through the guards' line anyway.

Guard #1 (with Sword)	5⚡5〰 ⊙9→⋲←8🛡
Guard #2 (with Sword)	6⚡9〰 ⊙3→⋲←9🛡
Guard #3 (with Sword)	9⚡2〰 ⊙7→⋲←1🛡

If you defeated the guards (#246).

#265

You firmly claim that you know the Citadel like the back of your hand, and if anyone can bring out such a treasure from there, it's you.

Knireek suspiciously sizes you up, then stands up without a word and clears a table in the darker part of the tavern by yanking two drunks slumped over the table to the floor and kicking them aside, then when he's done his job well, he sits down and gestures for you to join.

His two other companions stand up without a word, and one of them nods his head toward you, indicating that you should come too. You shrug and follow them to another table, which is also under an antler-decorated pillar and arched structure. On the pillar, you see this number engraved: 2-44

Knireek lowers his voice a bit and tells you that he believes you, but since you're new, you have to give something as collateral in exchange for your word, and then you can talk about the details afterward.

If you have 🧺**a large basket of fish** with you and leave it here as collateral (#25).

If you have 🧺**a hooded top** with you and leave it here as collateral (#323).

If you have 🧺**a leather glove** with you and leave it here as collateral (#79).

If you have 🧺**a vial of elixir** with you and leave it here as collateral (#226).

If you don't have any of these with you, or just don't trust them to leave anything with them, then you can simply stand up and walk back to the tavern counter (#195).

#266

You are running down a narrow street. The familiar scent of the sea is carried to you by the wind.

The guards are hot on your heels.

You can go forward from here (#335), or turn right (#364).

#267

If this is the first time you're trying with the coffin (#398), if you've already opened it before (#187).

#268

You learn that you've stumbled into the middle of the harvest festival, specifically the Empty Granary celebration. This is essentially one of the pre-harvest traditions, and some of them held — believe it or not — in the empty granary one or two days before the harvest begins.

There are surely already many people from the village here, as this is a grand feast that lasts well into the late evening.

You can ask if outsiders — like yourself — are allowed to attend the celebration (#303).

You can ask about Kiena if you haven't already (#82).

You can also go back to the marketplace, leaving the tavern behind (#6).

#269

The eerie haze of the battlefield clings to your thoughts like a shroud, the acrid stench of scorched earth and spilled blood thickening the air, making each breath feel labored and heavy. Shadows stretch long and twisted under a leaden sky, the distant echoes of crows picking at the fallen adding to the oppressive weight that urges you onward — you've glimpsed horrors enough to haunt your nights, so you force your legs into a hurried scramble up the hill's steep flank, the damp soil sucking at your boots with every step.

As you climb higher, the mist coils denser around the strewn corpses, their blue crests matted and dulled by congealing gore, when a peculiar glint pierces the gloom beside one lifeless form. At first, you dismiss it as sunlight fracturing through the haze on some discarded armor, but a insistent pull of curiosity — sharp and unbidden amid the suffocating dread — draws you closer, your heart pounding against the clammy chill. Peering through the swirling vapors, your hunch proves true: a exquisite little dagger emerges, its blade etched with faint, ethereal runes that pulse with an otherworldly blue luminescence, as if alive in the deadened fog.

If you want, you can take this 🗑 →|← **magical dagger** with you, ◯6→|←8🛡, you might find it very useful in later battles.

Besides that, you really feel that this cursed place holds nothing good for you, so you quicken your steps and, descending the other side of the hill, you follow the river again, this time downstream, which will lead you back exactly to the bridge where you left the road earlier (#91).

#270

You could inquire about work from the bartender (#285).

You could ask what they are celebrating (#190).

You could question him about local gossip (#117).

Or you could sit at one of the quiet tables, where someone is already slumped over, sleeping (#212), or perhaps join someone at another table, who is calmly sipping from their mug (#337).

#271

You are traveling on the path leading through the forest when in the distance you see two figures talking on the road. As you get closer, you see that you are dealing with guards who sullenly block your path, so it seems you can't go further this way.

You try to find out why there is this roadblock, but the gruff ones are not very talkative.

If you have ♀**a vial of charm potion** with you, you can use it here by subtracting the smaller number from the larger one and adding the resulting number to this chapter's number and continue reading there.

Failing that, however, you can go back toward 🗺**Moonward** on this road (#130).

#272

You place the gold on the tavern counter. Kokery smiles at the sight of the gleaming coin and nonchalantly reaches.

"I've never heard of her in my life, my friend!" he roars with laughter in his rumbling voice.

Hm (#313).

#273

You ask about Kiena, but he can't really help.

He thinks a bit, that he might have heard this name somewhere, perhaps in the city tavern during some stray gossip, but he didn't really pay attention to who exactly it could be.

He even asks back why you're looking for this person, to which you reply friendly that your common goal is to find the lost stones and perhaps together you could be more successful.

Jarse shrugs, he didn't know what kind of stones they could be, but they must be valuable if you're searching for them so persistently.

If you haven't done so yet, you can ask friendly what exactly he's doing here (#11), or you can find out what this big fuss is with the guarded city gates (#151).

Alternatively, you can say goodbye to him kindly, and continue on the path between the houses northward (#39), or head further west following the city wall (#238).

#274

You step over to the overturned grilling racks and start setting them up again over the fire to cook the fish on them. One of the villagers steps up to help you, and as you work on this, he introduces himself; his name is Buphas, and he's very grateful that a stranger is so self-lessly helpful.

Together, you almost immediately make the racks usable again over the fire, and now it's time for grilled fish!

You help them enthusiastically, but Buphas insists that you should rather lie down on the grass and enjoy the celebration, giving you one of the most beautifully grilled fish slices out of respect. You break off a piece of bread to go with it and start munching; this little break feels really good now, giving you **+3⚡** points.

While eating, you watch the cheerful villagers. They tirelessly revel and celebrate the upcoming harvest; you probably won't stay until the end of the celebration, but this little rest definitely feels good.

When you swallow the last bite, you slowly stand up, brush off the grass stuck to your clothes, and thank Buphas for his kindness. The young man starts blessing you openly, saying that actually he and the village owe you gratitude for your selflessness. With a sudden idea, he comes up with the plan that since the harvest is approach-ing, he will cut the first sheaf in your honor and for you. He grabs a sickle, and before you can blink twice, he has already cut a sheaf's worth, quickly ties it up for you, and hands it over with a smile.

You can't refuse his kindness, and you take this 🧺**sheaf of wheat** with you as the first honorary harvest. You thank him for his kindness once more, and then, disappearing behind the houses, you head back toward the marketplace.

It's just a short walk, and you're already there (#6).

#275

You struggle to move forward in the corridor, so it's particularly un-settling when the corridor simply ends.

> The mud reaches up to your knees, and you move heavily and uncertainly. You stumble and stagger, it's a miracle you can keep your balance. Roll two dice, and if the resulting number is greater than your 〰️ points, subtract **-1**⚡ from yourself as you stumble in the mud and fall, sustaining a minor injury.

It was clearly planned to carve more chambers into the ground, but for now, this branch of the corridor is a dead end.

From here, you can only go back to the chamber you came from (#378).

#276

The path leads straight to the city park, a very charming public gar-den surrounded by trees and small benches, bordered by beautiful yellow flowerbeds. The eastern edge of the park extends to the river-bank, but the river's dull, steady murmur can be heard almost every-where in the park.

You can walk down a narrow path to the riverbank (#9).

You can exit the park via the narrow street leading north (#387), or head west by crossing the bridge to the other side of the river (#169).

#277

After a few steps, the corridor offers a small choice of where to go next.

You can head northwest from here (#186).

One branch of the corridor leads east (#17).

To the south, you see the corridor narrowing, but by squeezing yourself, you can easily go that way too (#330).

#278

The door opens silently, and you step into what seems to be a parlor, certainly designed for ladies, judging by the colors and the embroidered decorations on the walls. The curtains are drawn open, and the sun's rays pleasantly warm the room. Beyond the large windows, the room has two exits.

You hear noises and voices from upstairs; you are not alone in the house! Roll two dice; if the result is greater than your 🖋 points, unfortunately, you failed to stay unnoticed and quiet, continue the story here (#13).

You can exit through the right-hand door (#64), or try the door opposite (#154).

#279

The small opening leads into a larger room; as you first look around, this could have once been used as a kitchen, at least judging by the presence of the stove and the large cutting table. On better days, the daily hot meal for the tower guards was probably prepared here.

However, now it has slowly become a musty and damp little room, moisture drips in drops from the walls, on the southern wall there is a huge and massive oak door, but as the walls have already sunk, the door is half underwater, and the iron straps reinforcing the door are visibly deformed and might have pierced into the ceiling and obviously into the floor as well, but this isn't exactly visible because of the water.

It could easily be that you won't be able to open this door easily or at all from here anymore, but why not try to force it anyway (#370).

On the wall opposite the small opening, you see only stacked shelves, perhaps it's worth looking at them closer (#333).

Alternatively, you can crawl back through the small opening toward the corridor from where you originally came, if you feel there's nothing interesting here (#191).

#280

You stand before the cells, a narrow confined corridor leads back to the chamber from where you came, and ahead of you, the passage ends exactly at two locked cells.

Faint lights filter in from somewhere above over the cells, but the cells themselves are deep underground, damp, and they stink from afar; in the northern cell, you see someone's dead body in the dim light.

If you have the 💡**cell key** with you, you can open the northern cell by writing the numbers on it next to each other, and adding them to this chapter's number, then continue reading there.

If you have the 💡**cell key** with you, you can open the southern cell by writing the numbers on it next to each other, and subtracting them from this chapter's number, then continue reading there.

If the cells no longer interest you, you can simply go back through the narrow corridor to the smaller chamber from where you came (#175).

#281

You immediately learn from the innkeeper that his name is Oreth, and he owns the only tavern here in 🗺 **Moonward**.

You can ask him about Kiena, perhaps he can tell you something about her (#76).

You can ask about the local wine as well (#357).

You can sit at an empty table, order something to eat and drink (#109).

You can inquire about the reasons for the reinforced guard (#200).

You can ask him for a room to rest temporarily (#18).

You can look around the tavern and take a closer look at the people drinking here (#395).

Or you can even leave the tavern and go back to the main square (#348).

#282

The tunnel narrows increasingly, but you still proceed comfortably — until you reach its end sealed with bars. Beyond the bars, you see a further cross-corridor, but there is neither a lock nor any visible mechanism on the bars that would open it.

You can go back from here to the junction (#23).

You can try to figure out how the bars can be opened (#54).

#283

Captain Davismore enthusiastically talks about how they've already sold a few crates, the fish are selling really well right now, they're still sorting the current catch, but if everything goes like this, they could set sail again in one or two days.

He says they won't return here with the next haul but will try their luck at 📖**Whitpoint**, as he's heard they pay very well for fresh goods there.

He'd love to chat more, but he has a lot to do, so for now, he wishes you good luck on your journey and in finding Kiena.

You can talk to Captain Rottora (#207).

Or if you're done here, you can head toward the fish market (#320) or the city marketplace (#181).

#284

The guards look at you strangely as you place all your weapons on the ground, but you know exactly that you must follow the instructions if you want the spell to work.

You step away from your weapons before slightly opening the vial. A bluish-purple vapor rises from it, immediately enveloping your weapons and those of the guards, and before they can react in any way, the purple cloud dissipates in the blink of an eye, and the two guards collapse to the ground, peacefully falling asleep.

You pick up your weapons from the ground and calmly continue walking north (#118).

#285

The bartender eyes you with a skeptical sneer after your cheery inquiry about work, his gaze lingering as if he's sizing up your face — or perhaps your true intentions. You quickly clarify, insisting nothing shady's on your mind.

He flashes a wry grin, sweeping a hand around the tavern's lively din. "Not exactly a hall of saints here," he quips with a casual shrug, his tone softening slightly.

With a grimace, he grumbles that the smithy might be worth a shot — Youngrek's been dawdling on forging new hinges for the tavern door, promised three weeks back but still undelivered. "Mind you," he adds, "I haven't paid him yet. Only a fool shells out coin before the work's done," laughs, but you are unsure where the actual joke is.

After a thoughtful pause, he muses that the carpenter's shop could be another lead. "Ifer's been scarce in town, likely roaming the woods for prime timber. A strapping lad like you might catch his eye for some labor."

You can ask what they are celebrating right now (#190).

You can ask what he knows about those not too honest and upright people he alluded to earlier (#14).

You can question him about local gossip (#117).

Or if you don't want to question him further, you can sit at one of the quiet tables, where someone is already slumped over sleeping (#212), or perhaps join someone at another table, who is peacefully sipping from their mug (#337).

#286

Wandering in the dense forest, you see white flowers to your right.

You can go left from here (#237), forward (#32), or even right (#137).

#287

You steel your nerves, ready to force the barred gate without a key. Gathering your strength, you hurl yourself against it, utterly unprepared for the hinges to tear free from the wall with such effortless surrender.

The entire gate wrenches out in one fluid motion, pitching you off balance; you stumble forward as the iron structure crashes down beneath you, momentum carrying it to the ground in a resounding thud.

It unfolds so swiftly that there's no chance to steady yourself before it's done. You glance up in wide-eyed surprise — not exactly as envisioned, but the path lies open all the same.

Rising to your feet, you dust yourself off, then carefully shift the gate aside in the corridor, making sure it won't hinder your way back.

From here, you can now go in three directions.

You can explore the corridor behind the newly opened recess heading south (#101).

You can continue east along this branch (#198).

You can go west back toward the statue (#239).

#288

The path continues through a smaller corridor from here, which, after a few minutes' walk, leads only to a junction. Any of the three directions could be good from here.

If you go northeast from here (#376), if you continue southeast (#175), or perhaps proceed along the northwest branch (#17).

#289

The path leads to a junction, where a massive stone bastion stands, it could be some kind of watchtower, and similarly abandoned as almost every corner of the village. Its thick oak door is slightly ajar.

You can try to enter the abandoned watchtower through the open door (#329).

You can go from here along the main street toward the tavern (#199).

As you look north from here, you can clearly see the source of the smoke column, a smaller house in the middle of a fenced farm. Directly next to and around the house, various sized small wooden boxes stand on legs. From here, you can go in that direction as well (#222).

#290

You head toward 📖**Whitpoint**, approaching the city, when you see that the bridge spanning the gorge, which would take you straight into the city, is completely collapsed. You go closer to the bridge to see what might have caused the bridge's destruction; from the signs, some kind of storm toppled the whole thing into the deep gorge.

It's certain that you can't get into the city via the bridge; you need to find some other path. The gorge looks quite steep; it doesn't really seem safe to climb down.

If you know 💡**any other way to the city**, you can find it by adding the product of the two numbers to this chapter's number, and continue the story there.

If you have no idea how to get into the city, then you have little choice left; only the way back to the junction seems safe at the moment (#159).

#291

The guards cast wary glances as you lay your weapons down with deliberate care, swords and daggers clinking softly on the stone, but you hold fast to the ritual's precise demands, knowing the spell's success hinges on compliance.

You glide back a step, deftly uncorking the vial just enough to release a swirling bluish-purple vapor that surges forth, coiling eagerly around your weapons and the guards' blades in a shimmering dance. Before their startled hands can move, the mist vanishes in a fleeting pulse, and the guards crumple gracefully to the ground, lulled into a serene slumber.

You can afford a light smirk.

You pick up your weapons from the ground and calmly continue walking north (#130).

#292

You offer your help in exchange for a few gold coins, but Ifer shakes his head, saying he can't afford to pay for helping hands right now, thanks you for trying, and trudges back to the saw-bench to continue his work.

Of course, you can still gladly offer him help without payment (#93).

Or you can leave Ifer and the workshop behind (#77).

#293

You ask directly if he would sell it to you if you paid for it. Obviously, the original owner paid its price, but of course, you're also willing to pay good gold for it. You see him thinking, then he agrees, perhaps you can do business; he's looking for a gift for his daughter's wedding, something shiny, valuable.

> If you have a heart-shaped key decorated with a green gem, you can offer it to him in exchange for the bow, and you can take the 🧺 →|← **light bow** with ⊙**10** →|← **6** 🛡, which you might find very handy in any battle.

Either way, you can ask him about Kiena if you haven't already (#298).

Or you can say goodbye and set off on your way. A path leads north from here (#156), or you can go west following the city wall (#356).

#294

You weave through the smaller streets until you find the house the thieves mentioned. It's indeed quite a charming little mansion, hopefully with no one home right now. The house and its surroundings are quiet, likely because everyone is at the main square's bustle.

You can try sneaking in through the main entrance (#64), or through the back garden (#386).

#295

You arrive in a smaller chamber with an ornate stone floor, and almost exactly in the center of the room, there is a small pile of rubble.

If this is the first time you're here (#332), if you've already been here (#136).

#296

You've had enough of the skeletons for a while; as you hurry back, a small bag attached to one of the saddles catches your eye, as if there's something in it. You step over and carefully open it, unsure of what might be inside; to your greatest surprise, it's some kind of scroll.

As you carefully unroll it, you see that it might be a map of the dungeons beneath some kind of bastion or watchtower.

This could definitely be useful; if you want to put away the 🧺**watchtower map (2-6)**, then maybe it's time to leave this cursed area behind you (#269).

#297

The trees and bushes grow denser around you, and soon the path leads right through the heart of the forest; for now, you see nothing on the road, neither nearby nor far off.

You can continue westward (#156) or go eastward (#106).

#298

He thinks a little, then shakes his head, saying he hasn't heard this name yet, but in the city at the tavern, Oreth has surely heard of her; he knows something about everything that happens in the area and also about those who have been here.

According to him, you should ask him. You nod, saying that you will definitely try your luck with him, because you really want to find Kiena.

You can also ask him about the weapons he's currently working on (#86), if you haven't already.

Or you can set off on your way: a path leads north from here (#156), or you can go west following the city wall (#356).

#299

As you step into the cell, the dead body visibly starts to stir, and a moment later, you find yourself facing a quite unpleasant skeleton warrior.

There's no choice; you have to put him in his place.

Skeleton (with Sword)	28 ⚡3 🗡 ⊙6 →⊩3 🛡

If you defeated the skeleton, then afterward you quickly glance around the cell, but you don't really find anything interesting here; you look up at the small opening filtering in from above, which can barely be wider than your fist — it would be completely hopeless to escape from here through it.

However, a slight breath of fresh air filters in through it, which in some strange way you can particularly appreciate right now.

Beyond that, there's really no way out from here except back the way you came (#280).

#300

You quickly climb up the ladder back to the pantry, where practically nothing has changed.

The ceiling trapdoor is still too high, and you certainly won't be able to open it from here, however, the trapdoor on the floor stands open before you, and the ladder leads back to the wine cellar (#388).

If you wish, you can also go from here through the kitchen toward the corridor from where you originally came (#191).

#301

The founding of the Citadel seems to have begun with the construction of a single large stone house, back in the time of the first founder, Gaki Chakgrek, and it served primarily as protection against the stormy sea weather. The story mentions that even in the founding era, it became Gaki's own residence, and it remained his until death.

O ur eternal support inhabits these walls, outstanding in devotion and honor. We all bow in agreement. We dedicate it to him deservedly and in old age as his grave and beyond.

We bow our heads and kneel before this place, remembering what he did and forgetting the bloody moments, drawing gratitude from his memory, and we do this for our children and their children.

Thus, over time, it became a memorial, and a later chapter mentions that it was converted into a temple, an altar was placed in it, where Gaki received an eternal sanctuary.

M emories are strong, a sad era comes eventually. Only Gaki could draw strength into us. His strong hands and will made our people what we are today. We must sacrifice for his spirit so that it remains with us forever, and his spirit accompanies us now and beyond.

The great ones are all destined to be remembered, and required to be honored. With pure intent, we establish a place here, and we remember and honor. We carry it forward and teach it. A single rose is capable of wonders.

After this, the Citadel belonged only to the city for a long time; in later centuries, it grew and turned into a cult site over the years, expanded countless times to accommodate newer and newer altars. It seems the Citadel became a kind of burial place, as a contemporary writing mentions when taking stock of the altars erected in the Citadel.

Some forty-odd altars have been placed in the Citadel and its dungeons over the years, in honor and memory of the eternal leaders. The main altar is still Gaki's, the eternal founder's, but his altar was also relocated multiple times during the expansions.

Later ~ not very distinguished ~ rulers also received places in the underground catacombs, honoring and displaying value, their graves were most often piled with gold and precious stones, to give worthy value after their death to their wretched reigns.

Thus, rich treasures can also be found in the catacombs and underground dungeons. Unless they have already been looted, in any case, it's completely understandable why the Citadel is surrounded by such protection.

If you wish, you can read more on other topics about the Citadel (#114), or simply stop reading and try further in the fresh air (#77).

#302

As you glide toward the platform, the group's brash boasts ripple through the air, their voices dripping with swagger as they flash gold coins, promising rich payment to anyone presenting an item of value — provided they can't counter with something even grander.

You sense a sliver of truth in their bold claims, yet intuition whispers they're cunningly fishing for the town's hidden treasures, likely scheming to pilfer them under the cloak of an unwatched night.

They now brandish a dagger encrusted with gleaming gemstones, its blade catching the light as they challenge the crowd, daring anyone to produce something finer and vowing to buy it on the spot.

If you have a 💡**sword inlaid with red precious stones** with you, you can show it to them by adding the two numbers and subtracting from this chapter's number, then continue reading there.

If you have a 💡**golden statuette** with you, you can show it to them by multiplying the two numbers and adding to this chapter's number, then continue reading there.

If you feel that you can't or don't want to show them anything now, then perhaps you can visit the tavern on the other side of the square (#216).

Or you can leave this bustle toward the southwest-lying harbor (#96), or even follow the narrower street behind the platform northeastward (#387).

#303

Kokary says that of course anyone can go to the celebration; villagers are constantly coming and going from the tavern, and he gestures to a small group heading toward the granary, inviting you to join them if you feel like it (#138).

But you can stay and ask about Kiena (#82).

Or you can go back to the marketplace, leaving the tavern behind (#6).

#304

The local blacksmith is working enthusiastically but stops as you approach and greets you warmly, introducing himself as Elliniar, the village smith. He's currently working on lances and spears for the local guards — not the most exiting weapons, but it pays well, especially now that the guards are patrolling day and night everywhere around here (#162).

#305

You rush down a narrow street, with the city walls towering over you on your right.

The guards are hot on your heels.

You can go right from here (#264), or run forward along the narrow street (#362).

#306

You step over the scattered bones and cautiously peer through the open lid of the coffin — seeing nothing new that you haven't already seen.

That wasn't very interesting this time (#329).

#307

"Your efforts will not go unpaid," he tosses a pouch toward you, then retreats into his hut.

You open it and find **12**⊛ inside. Not bad for a jar of honey.

You can try to coax him out again (#70), or if you think it's time to return to the main road, you can leave this strange hut and its occupant behind (#50).

#308

You walk into a vast chamber, likely one of the storage rooms.

> The mud reaches up to your knees, and you move heavily and uncertainly. You stumble and stagger, it's a miracle you can keep your balance. Roll two dice, and if the resulting number is greater than your 🐿 points, subtract **-1⚡** from yourself as you stumble in the mud and fall, sustaining a minor injury.

The chamber has exits in three directions.

To your left, a path leads through a smaller corridor (#353).

Moving forward, the outline of another smaller chamber comes into view (#168).

While in the opposite direction, you see another mud-covered chamber where an altar stands (#224).

#309

You kneel by the chest and try to open it.

If this is the first time you're opening the chest (#361), if you've already opened it before (#2).

#310

You run down a narrow little street, the scent of the sea growing stronger, and you believe you can see the masts from here already. However, you can't figure out which path will lead you to the harbor from here.

If you have ♀a map of 🗺Whitpoint's secret streets with you, you can use it here by multiplying the middle digit by itself, adding the two other numbers, then adding the resulting value to this chapter's number, and continue the story there.

The guards are panting on your heels.

You can go left from here (#369), or forward (#346).

#311

The altar has obviously been desecrated.

And this is still the mildest way to express how ugly and aggressively it was looted and its valuables stolen over time. One cannot even imagine how splendid it must have been in its heyday; now, really, only the empty stone slab remains — due to its worthlessness and weight, no one had the idea to take it from here — and of course, the altar's rear ornately carved stone slab was also here, although as seen from the signs and the huge cracks, someone has already tried to smash this too.

Exactly for what purpose is a mystery, since the carved patterns themselves show that if the stone slab is whole — undoubtably someone else realized this too, that's why they might have stopped halfway in breaking the stone slab into pieces, but still caused very serious damage to it before giving up. In its current state, really only the multi-point attachment to the ingeniously engineered rock wall holds it together. The broken pieces could even be pried off one by one, if someone perhaps needed smaller pieces of the decoration.

You would like to examine the altar's ornate rear wall more closely (#21).

Alternatively, you can examine the rotting benches, if you're interested in such things (#146).

If you've seen enough, you can choose the only exit as well, north along the corridor (#101).

#312

Your obvious intentions do not go unnoticed; two guards rush toward you with their lances. From here, you have few choices left; you must defeat them if you want to enter the city.

Guard #1 (with Sword)	8 ⚡ 4 🌀 ⊙4 →∣← 7 🛡
Guard #2 (with Sword)	6 ⚡ 6 🌀 ⊙5 →∣← 6 🛡

If you win the battle (#22).

#313

He pivots away, deftly pouring half a mug of frothy beer before swinging back to face you, his eyes narrowing as he leans in close. In a hushed tone, he murmurs a warning to tread lightly with such bold questions — strangers probing too eagerly or flaunting their wits often stir unease among the villagers. For him, it's all good trade; secrets swapped across the bar bring a tidy trickle of coin, but he urges you to soften your approach as an outsider. That is probably the most useful advice anyone could give you recently.

Still, he confides that Kiena passed through a few weeks back, bartering her strength to mend a local shed in exchange for a bed. He himself housed her, yet one morning she slipped away without a word. Cocking his head, he asks if you're her friend, and you give a hesitant nod, admitting you've never met her but heard she's the only one who can track down the lost stones you seek.

Kokary's brow lifts, curiosity glinting as he presses for details about the stones. You flash a sly smile, quipping that in your tavern, such tales come with a price. At that, he throws back his head with a booming laugh, clapping your shoulder with warm approval, though his grin suggests he's not about to pay for your secrets.

But he continues by saying that as far as he heard from the villagers' gossip, Kiena headed toward 🗺**Whitpoint** from here — but whether this is truly true or just empty chatter, he can't tell you.

Despite he is probably the most weird innkeeper you even met, he can't tell you more about Kiena than that.

You can still ask about the particularly great bustle in the village (#268).

Or you can leave the tavern and go back to the marketplace (#6).

#314

"Oh, fish... Well, the fish market (#320) is that way," the armored man points forward, "you can buy and sell fish there, stranger, you'll surely get a good price for your goods when the ships come in with fresh stock, as that's when the servants from the Citadel come to shop, and it's easy to get a good price."

#315

You're running down the main street, this section of the main street completely deserted right now.

The guards are hot on your heels.

You can continue along the main street (#358), or turn left onto a smaller street (#266).

#316

You simply make your way through the grated door laid on the ground next to the small recess. You still can't believe how easily you were able to open it.

From here, you can go in three directions.

Along the branch behind the small recess southward (#101).

You can go east from here (#198).

You can go west from here (#239).

#317

It occurs to you that you have a map of a watchtower; perhaps you can make use of it here. You take it out, and it seems you're on the right track — the map probably depicts this tower, along with all its secret passages. You look around, then search for the stone embedded in the wall that opens the secret passage at the marked location. As you press the stone slightly forward, the passage opens before you with a small rumble, revealing a spiral staircase leading downward, likely to the lower levels of the tower.

You cautiously start walking down the stairs; you might be halfway when you hear a dry rattling sound from below, and you see a skeleton trying to come up the stairs. It hasn't noticed you yet; if you want to turn back, you can quietly return to the upper level (#329), or face the skeleton on your way down.

Skeleton (with Sword)	19⚡7〰 ⊙3→∣←3🛡

If you defeated the skeleton, then you continue your way downward, all the way until you reach the bottom of the stairs (#263).

#318

In the dining room, there's nothing else to see; the pieces of the previously shattered vase are no longer here, only a wet spot in the middle of the table hints at how clumsy you were earlier.

The dining room has two exits; you can go right from here (#386) or choose the other door (#278).

#319

You ease back into the chair beside the figure slumped over the table, still lost in a peaceful slumber after you discreetly lightened his pockets moments ago. His head has shifted slightly, now facing the other way, oblivious to the world.

A plate before him holds a few uneaten morsels of cheese and roast meat, abandoned mid-meal. You linger there, the tavern's warm hum wrapping around you, when your gaze drifts to the trio at the next table — those who earlier beckoned you to join them — still huddled close, their voices weaving a secretive murmur.

If you know 💡**who they are and what they're plotting**, then you can sit down with them by multiplying the two numbers under the antler decorating the pillar and subtracting from this chapter's number, and continue at the resulting chapter.

But you can sit over to one of the solitary drinkers at another table (#337).

Or if you've had enough of tavern loitering, you can go back to the city (#143).

#320

The fish market indeed has everything related to fish or seafood. Including two things: the stench of fish and the raucous screeching of seagulls. But in return, the sun shines beautifully, and perhaps because of that, or perhaps due to the abundance of fresh goods, it seems there's a lot of interest and bustling today.

It will be easy to sell fish here today.

If you have a 🧺**large basket of fish** with you, you can try to sell it here for **9**✲.

There's not much else to see beyond this; a direct path leads to the marketplace from here (#181), you can navigate through the small paths behind the houses to Youngrek (#220), or if you're ready to set off, you can look for a ship in the harbor (#49) that can take you on board.

#321

You remember from the map that another smaller room opens from the kitchen, perhaps it was the pantry back then, or something like that. Behind the remnants of the shelves, you spot the door leading to the small pantry; it seems this one isn't stuck, and as you push it, it gives way easily, accompanied by a small creak.

The room you enter is very small; you see a trapdoor on the ceiling, but you certainly won't be able to open it from here; however, the trapdoor on the floor gives way easily, and it seems that a small ladder leads downward from here.

The ladder doesn't look very trustworthy, but perhaps it will hold if you think you want to go down (#388).

If you wish, you can go back through the kitchen toward the corridor from where you originally came, if that seems safer (#191).

#322

You politely thank him for his kindness and, leaving the house, walk back to the first crossroad where you can decide where to go next: south along the narrow street (#276), or toward the rumbling sound, walking down the southwest street (#107).

#323

You set the top on the table with a playful flourish, and Knireek's eyes widen before he erupts in a booming laugh, pounding his chest armor with a clang that echoes through the tavern. He grins, clearly tickled by your jest, but declares with a mock-serious shake of his head that he wouldn't swap his sturdy breastplate for a rag that'd barely fend off a breeze. His two companions, catching the quip, throw their heads back in raucous, wheezing guffaws, their laughter bouncing off the walls like a contagious chorus.

He pats your shoulder, saying it was a clever try, but he has no use for junk.

If you have 🧺**a large basket of fish** with you and leave it here as collateral (#25).

If you have 🧺**a leather glove** with you and leave it here as collateral (#79).

If you have 🧺**a vial of elixir** with you and leave it here as collateral (#226).

If you don't have any of these with you, or just don't trust them to leave anything with them, you can simply stand up and walk back to the tavern counter (#195).

#324

Wandering in the dense forest, you see white flowers to your left and spot a few freshly cut trunks to your right.

You can go left from here (#254), or even right (#92).

#325

You take the sword in hand and slide the blade between the door hinges and the wall; the lowest hinge, underwater, snaps easily, but you struggle a bit with the second hinge, pressing the blade harder, then you hear the metal snap, and you smile.

> Your joy is short-lived, as instead of the hinge rivets, a small piece breaks off from your sword's blade. You look at the forged iron disappointedly; this is not a good sign. This means **-2** points from your sword's current damage value.

You can try to push against the door with your shoulder (#94).

Or you can walk back to the spiral staircase (#263).

#326

The corridor goes in one direction for a while, then widens slightly and makes a sharp turn, almost at a right angle. There's absolutely nothing at the turn; the corridor simply changes direction, seemingly for no reason.

You can go northeast from here (#234).

You can go southeast from here (#183).

#327

You mention Freela's name to him and that you came regarding a potion.

He kindly invites you into his hut, placing some cheese and bread before you, which you start to nibble on. As you sit there, Jarse brings out a small vial and places it meaningfully on the table in front of you. He explains that this is what Freela asked him for, and of course, since he sees that you two are also good friends, he doesn't mind if you take it to her, especially since she already requested it.

Jarse brings out the vial containing the essential oil and asks for **5**✸ in exchange. If you have that much gold and want to pay for it (#166).

You can try to haggle, perhaps he'll give it to you for **3**✸ (#104).

If you don't want to or can't pay for it (#44).

#328

You notice Ifer's weary frame relax with a moment's rest, so you ease into conversation, sharing that you're a recent arrival in search of Kiena, rumored to be lingering somewhere in the city. Ifer shakes his head gently, his brow furrowing. "Never heard of a traveler by that name," he admits, "but I'm rarely at the city tavern, so it might've slipped past me."

He shrugs, unable to offer any leads on Kiena's whereabouts.

Curious, you steer the talk toward the city itself, and Ifer's tone grows lively. He reveals that troublemakers have been plaguing the streets lately, prompting the guards to bar strangers from the city center. This irks Bukatiz, the local bartender, who's been vocal about the loss of trade — travelers rarely reach his tavern for drinks or lodging now. "He's raised a fuss more than once," Ifer says with a wry smile, "but the guards won't budge. Too many thefts targeting the Citadel."

He muses that when winter's chill arrives, the strange faces might dwindle, possibly coaxing the guards to reopen the gates. As for the Citadel, Ifer's eyes glint knowingly. "It's brimming with gemstones and gold — small wonder it draws thieves like moths to a flame. But with strangers kept out, the attempts have thinned, and the guards pounce on any would-be robbers with fierce resolve."

You'd talk more, but work awaits Ifer; you can try to agree with him that in exchange for a few gold coins, you'll help him (#292) in the absence of his apprentice.

Or you can leave him here and walk back to the street (#77), and continue there.

#329

You are in the ground-floor foyer of the tower; this is a circular, continuous room with a spiral staircase in the middle leading upward from here. Opposite the entrance, against the wall, on a very low stone altar lies a closed wooden coffin.

> If you have 💡**the watchtower map** with you, you can use it here now by multiplying the two numbers on the map and subtracting from this chapter's number, then continue at the resulting chapter.

But you can go upward from here on the spiral staircase (#214).

Or you can examine the coffin (#256).

You can exit the tower if you're done here (#51).

#330

The corridor doesn't get wider, but suddenly it opens into a spacious chamber, in the middle of which stands a fountain, and not only does it stand there, but despite being overgrown with vines, it is currently functioning.

From here, you can't quite see what's in the farther, darker corner of the chamber, but the pleasant sound of water splashing could be inviting. You can go deeper into the chamber to explore every corner (#81).

Or if you think you've seen enough, you can go back through the narrow corridor all the way to the junction (#277).

#331

You step out of the mill, and instead of taking the winding dirt path, you cut through the wheat fields back toward the city. You don't have to walk long downhill from the hill, where, after taking a shorter curve around the village and the houses, you sharply turn south.

The road isn't far from the field, and after jumping over a couple of ditches, you soon find yourself on the dirt road leading toward 📖**Dispel**. A few clouds are currently blocking the sun from you, but it seems that within minutes it will emerge again from behind the small puff.

As you approach the city, the golden-yellow wheat fields along the road gradually thin out, and even before you can see Youngrek's smithy in the distance, the gently swaying crops have disappeared from the roadside.

In the distance, the city's outlines gradually come into sharper focus, you can follow that path (#220).

#332

You step carelessly into the chamber, activating some hidden mechanism by stepping on one of the ornate stones, and from the direction of the southern wall, you hear three successive, quick, and sharply whistling sounds. By the time you realize, two spikes have already whizzed past you and embedded into the opposite wall; however, the third such thick spike embeds into your thigh, which you experience accompanied by sharp pain.

This little carelessness means **-3⚡** points for you now.

You try to figure out what would be the good solution: whether to bandage the wound as it is with the spike in your leg (#28) or first pull out the spike from your leg and only then bandage the bleeding wound (#103).

#333

Someone was searching for something here, and it seems they left behind the empty shelves toppled over in great anger. They visibly completely barricaded the wall.

> If you have 💡**a map of the watchtower** with you, then you can remember that another room opens from the kitchen from here, where you can get to by multiplying the two numbers on the map and subtracting from this chapter's number, and continue there.

Otherwise, there's not much to see; you can try to force the thick oak door if you haven't yet (#370).

Or from here, you can crawl back through the small opening toward the corridor from where you originally came, if you feel there's nothing interesting here (#191).

#334

"Do you need strength to win?" he asks, to which you nod.

> At that moment, some kind of lightning-like force strikes you, knocking you to the ground; for a short time, you can't feel your limbs and are unable to move. Subtract **-4**⚡ points from yourself, if you survive the strike, continue.

As you slowly start to come to and are able to move again, you stand up and dust yourself off. Whoever this mysterious figure was, they significantly strengthened you; add **+6**🦵 points to it.

You're somewhere in the middle of the forest, with no trace of the hut or the enigmatic hooded figure. Hesitantly, you start walking in one direction, hoping to find your way out from here (#237).

#335

You are running down a narrow little street, the scent of the sea is getting stronger, and you believe you can already see the masts from here. However, you can't see at all which path will take you to the harbor from here.

> If you have 💡a map of 📖Whitpoint's secret streets with you, you can use it here by multiplying the two last digits, adding the smallest number, then adding the resulting value to this chapter's number, and continue the story there.

The guards are panting on your heels.

You can go left from here (#310), or right (#364).

#336

"Your reward will not go unpaid," he tosses a pouch toward you, then retreats into his hut.

You open it and find **3**✸ inside.

Hm. You hoped for a bit more for this fine wine.

You can try to coax him out again (#70), or if you think it's time to return to the main road, you can leave this strange hut and its occupant behind (#50).

#337

You settle onto a creaky wooden chair at a table where a lone man hunches, nursing a tarnished tankard of ale with a bitter scowl, his cloak a faded russet that seems to soak up the dim tavern glow. His eyes, shadowed under a mop of chestnut hair, don't flicker your way as you sit; instead, he dives headlong into a woeful tale, his voice thick with sorrow. He recounts how his heart's darling, sweet Angene, radiant in her wedding gown of shimmering ivory and sapphire lace, fled from the altar's sacred vow, perhaps into the arms of a mysterious stranger — a figure cloaked in enigma he'd never glimpsed before — leaving him drowning in crimson shame beneath the vibrant garlands of their would-be wedding day.

It's an interesting and heartbreaking story, and of course, if possible, you'd be curious to hear Angene's perspective on it (5-61), if you ever bump into her.

You listen to him for a while longer, trying to offer wise platitudes to help, but he doesn't really listen to anything, just keeps repeating his own misery, and after a while, it feels like you're hearing the same story for the hundredth time.

You can try talking to the bartender instead (#195).

Or you can move to another table where someone is peacefully sleeping (#212).

#338

Wandering in the dense forest, you see white flowers to your left.

You can go left from here (#286), or even right (#254).

#339

You cautiously rummage through the small pile of hay with your foot, unsure what you're hoping to find — bones, or perhaps something more useful — but as you sift through the hay, you feel a sharp sting in your leg. You hiss in pain and then see that a snake has bitten you!

You can only hope it wasn't a venomous snake and that you'll survive the bite. Angrily, you kick the creature to the ground, stomping and hitting it until it stops moving. Then you feel yourself growing weaker and collapse to the ground; this little carelessness costs you **-10** ⚡ points, and if you still alive, you will only need to deduct this until you reach a doctor who can somehow treat you.

At that point, you automatically regain the ⚡ points lost here, make a note of that.

It takes a few minutes to partially recover your strength and stand up again.

If you're still in an adventurous mood, you can take a look at the wooden chest (#85).

Or you can leave this unlucky cell behind (#280).

#340

The tavern is not far from here, just a few steps away.

The tavern door swings wide, its weathered oak frame beckoning weary travelers with an inviting embrace, while above it, a sign painted in bold crimson and gold proclaims Freela's Inn in swirling, flamboyant script. Without a pause, you stride through the threshold, drawn by the lively hum within, and make your way to the bar.

Behind the counter stands a fiery sprite of a bartender, her auburn hair catching the lantern light like a halo of embers, her eyes sparkling with mischief. You try to gauge if she runs this bustling haven solo, but no commanding figure in rugged boots or broad shoulders looms nearby — only guests, men and women alike, savoring hearty plates of roast and clinking mugs of frothy ale in the tavern's warm, amber glow.

You step up to the counter to greet her, but all you get in return for your friendly words is a curt head toss.

If you have **2**⊛ in your pouch, you can order a small mug of cider and try to strike up a conversation with the lively barmaid (#150).

Or you can walk out of the tavern, leaving the unfriendly atmosphere behind (#394).

#341

At first glance, the statue seems unremarkable, its weathered stone blending into the dim chamber, but as you draw nearer, a faint whistle of air hums from beneath its base, hinting it's not fully anchored to the pedestal. You press a hand against its cool surface, sensing its heft but also its surprising give — light enough to tilt with effort. Emboldened, you push harder, nudging the statue until it leans precariously against the room's cramped wall, teetering but held by the tight space, revealing a narrow gap beneath its base.

You lean cautiously toward the opening, curiosity piqued, when a sharp crack splits the air — a spear lurches upward from the gap, halting half-exposed with a jarring clank. The trap, poorly set, misses you entirely, its threat reduced to a heart-stopping jolt that freezes your breath for a beat. Dust swirls from the triggered mechanism, and you wave it away, coughing softly as it clouds your vision.

As the haze clears, a glint catches your eye — something dangles from the spear's tip. You reach out gingerly, unhooking a delicate gold chain, its links gleaming faintly in the torchlight, cradling a compass that shimmers with a golden sheen. Inspecting it, you notice the needle spins wildly, refusing to settle north or anywhere, twirling ceaselessly as you tilt the curious relic in your hand.

If you want, you can put away the 🧺**gold chain with the hanging compass (4-28)**; it might even be that, although it has no practical value, due to its shine, you could get a few gold coins for it from some merchant.

There's not much more to see around the statue, but from the chamber, you can proceed in two directions from here.

You can go south from here (#23).

You can go east, where the passage continues in a narrow tunnel; here, you'll only be able to proceed by crawling (#89).

#342

You keep running down a narrow street.

The guards are hot on your heels.

You can go left from here (#369), or run forward toward the main street (#243).

#343

As you proceed along the road, in the far distance you spot a small hut by the roadside. As you get closer, you see that its roof is half collapsed, and not all of its walls are still standing. It might have once been an inn by the junction, judging from the half-hanging sign that the gentle breeze still tosses back and forth, but for now, it seems completely uninhabited and abandoned.

Looking at the junction's signpost, you can go in three directions from here.

North toward 📖 **Dispel**, as indicated by the sign (#123).

East — or rather, southeast — a narrower branch indicates 📖 **Kadedh** (#55).

South still points to Dig, but that's well beyond the country's borders. Nevertheless, you can continue in that direction (#225).

#344

The lumberjacks' company seems interesting; you confidently step over and ask if you can join them. The three-person group pauses their conversation for a moment, then gestures that of course you can join if you feel like it.

You happily sit among them, mentioning that you're new in the city and looking for someone. They look at you curiously but seem willing to help if they can.

You can ask them if they've heard of Kiena (#393).

You can ask them about the forests around the city (#184).

Or if these don't interest you, you can talk to the bartender instead (#281).

#345

As you step closer to the altar, the altar begins to glow more intensely with a bluish otherworldly light, and as you reach for the flowers, the bluish light strongly pushes you away and keeps you at a distance from the altar. You try again, but it's as if you hit a solid wall after a certain point, and you can't reach the flowers..

You also try to poke them out with your sword, but you have the exact same feeling, as if some invisible wall stands between you and the altar.

You have no idea how you could take the blue flowers from the altar (#224).

#346

You can't proceed forward from here; however, the smaller company of guards chasing behind you has easily caught up to you in this dead end. You must fight them anyway if you want to continue your path toward the harbor.

Guard #1 (with Sword)	5⚡5🌀 ⊙9→|←8🛡
Guard #2 (with Sword)	6⚡9🌀 ⊙3→|←9🛡
Guard #3 (with Sword)	9⚡2🌀 ⊙7→|←4🛡

If you defeated the guards (#264).

#347

You walk along a wide road lined with trees; everything seems peaceful, and apart from the pleasant chirping of birds, there's not much else to see here. You don't see any junctions, yet you come across a signpost indicating 🗺**Houdmins** to the north (#380) and 🗺**Whitpoint** to the south (#159).

#348

You stand in the small town's main square; the bustle isn't too lively at this hour of the day. From here, you can see both city gates, one leading east and the other west.

On the opposite side of the square, you see a tavern; it might be worth visiting (#5).

But you could also leave the town through either the eastern gate (#156) or the western gate (#20).

#349

You order a bottle of wine from the bartender for the table, and you immediately steal your way into the heart of the company; the laughter and drinking soon bear fruit, as the wine diminishes from the bottle, they talk more freely about all sorts of topics, when one of them gestures everyone closer as if preparing to share a great secret with you.

When you all lean closer, he begins whispering.

"I know where the bartender keeps the wine..." he pauses for a longer dramatic effect. "In the wine cellar!" he bursts into laughter, and a moment later, you all join in the merriment. Then he gestures everyone closer again, calls for silence, and starts anew.

"Let's steal some," he says determinedly, then begins to describe how he's already scoped out that a secret entrance leads to the cellar through the back courtyard (4-33); however, getting there is quite difficult, only possible from the back street behind the tavern, but that's right across from the guards' quarters, and they'll immediately notice if someone tries to climb over the fence.

You're in an adventurous mood and a bit tipsy too, so you slam the table firmly, declaring that you'll bring some of that wine, come hell or high water. The others cheer loudly at your determination, you pour the last drops into the glasses, then you gulp it down and promise that you won't return here until the wine is in your hand.

It might be time to talk to the bartender (#281).

Or if you feel you've had enough to drink, you can even step out of the tavern for some fresh air (#348).

#350

You take a step toward the bookshelf when the floor creaks loudly under your foot; this was surely audible even from upstairs (#13).

#351

What you didn't notice at first glance becomes unmistakably shimmering with a greenish light in one corner of the chamber on second glance. It could be a trap, but it might also be worth the risk to find out what it is.

You cautiously approach the shimmer and see that it's indeed a kind of key, adorned with a heart-shaped green gemstone. You can't tell how much it might be worth, but if you wish, you can take the 🧺 **heart-shaped key decorated with a green gemstone** with you.

If you'd rather leave the chamber, you can go northwest through a smaller corridor (#326), or walk through the arched opening into another chamber very similar to this one (#295).

#352

Wandering in the dense forest, you spot the outlines of a hut. Bluish-purple smoke rises from its chimney; you're completely sure that you'll be dealing with some kind of magic, since such smoke doesn't exist naturally.

You can also go closer to the hut to find out what's hidden here (#70).

If you decide instead that this is too risky and turn back anyway (#50).

#353

You trudge through a mud-covered corridor until you reach a T-shaped junction.

> The mud reaches up to your knees, making it quite difficult and unsteady to move. You stumble and stagger, it's a miracle you can keep your balance. Roll two dice, and if the resulting number is greater than your 〰 points, subtract **-1**⚡ from yourself as you stumble in the mud and fall, sustaining a minor injury.

From this junction, you can head toward the circular, partially cleared chamber (#56).

You can continue your path in the right-hand branch of the corridor (#308).

Or you can head left, where you sense a larger chamber looming (#4).

#354

You gesture to the person you spoke with earlier to come behind the platform, then pull the golden statue from your pouch. You see his eyes light up as he reaches for his purse.

"I promised a good price, my friend," he says, taking one of the purses in hand without even opening it, and hands it to you. "What do you say to **25**✹?"

This is far more than you expected, so you accept without blinking. You hand him the statue, and without a word, you both go about your own business.

You can head to the tavern on the other side of the square for a drink (#216), or leave this circus toward the southwest-lying harbor (#96), or with less attention, follow the narrower street behind the platform northeastward (#387).

#355

You're trudging along the road at the city's outskirts; to the west, you see a forest (#158), while the road continues eastward into the city's main street (#169).

#356

You walk past the houses, bypassing the grim city walls; the houses are uniform until you spot a cottage blessed with a strikingly ornate gate.

As you step closer, the door opens, and a hooded figure steps out, then stops and looks around. When he notices you, he waves friendly.

"What brings you this way?" he greets warmly.

> If perhaps 💡**Freela sent you**, you can tell him so by adding the two numbers, then subtracting the result from this chapter's number, and continue reading there.

You can ask him friendly what exactly he's doing here (#11).

You can ask him about Kiena too, perhaps he knows something (#273).

You can inquire what this big fuss is with the guarded city gates (#151).

Alternatively, you can continue here on the path between the houses northward (#39), or head further west following the city wall (#238).

#357

Oreth tells you that it's not exactly local wine; it originally comes from around 🗺**Kadedh**. The last shipment arrived a few weeks ago, and apparently, the barrels spent decades underground untouched, with time maturing them to such splendor.

He tells you that he'd be happy to serve you a mug, just find an empty table, and he'll be at your service (#109).

You can ask him about Kiena, perhaps he can tell you something about her (#76).

You can inquire about the reasons for the reinforced guard (#200).

You can ask him for a room to rest temporarily (#18).

You can look around the tavern and take a closer look at the people drinking here (#395).

Or you can even leave the tavern and go back to the main square (#348).

#358

You're running down the main street; as far as you can see, the road leads straight to the city's southern gate from here. The gates are completely lowered.

The guards are hot on your heels.

You can continue along the main street (#246), turn left onto a smaller street (#26), or sharply turn back left onto an even narrower street (#266).

#359

You are traveling on the path leading through the forest when in the distance you see two figures talking on the road. As you get closer, you see that you are dealing with guards who sullenly block your path, saying that you can't go further this way.

You try to find out why there is this roadblock, but the guards are not very talkative.

> If you have 💡**a vial of charm potion** with you, you can use it here by multiplying the two numbers and subtracting from this chapter's number, and continue reading there.

Failing that, however, you can go back toward 📖**Houdmins** on this road (#118).

#360

You take out the golden compass and firmly place it on the platform floor as a challenger. The crowd starts buzzing even louder, as they compare them, they click their tongues satisfied and loudly proclaim that this time too, a more valuable item has been shown.

He lifts the compass above his head, and loudly shouts that the audience can see another masterpiece, and he's willing to pay even **15**✸ for it. It's up to you whether you accept the offer and want to sell the compass to them for that much.

Either way, one of them discreetly invites you behind the platform, and at the moment, you don't really know what to expect from them if you accept the invitation (#141).

If you feel that you're not interested in what they have to say, you can leave them and go across the square to the tavern (#216), down one street toward the southwest-lying harbor (#96), or perhaps follow the narrower street behind the platform northeastward (#387).

#361

You slowly open the chest, surprised that it's not locked, and the lid almost pops open on its own.

As you glimpse the contents of the chest and the single item inside, it immediately becomes clear — this is exactly the one thing you came to the Citadel for: the purple gemstone. As you take the gemstone, you instantly feel its magical effect, just as mysteriously as Knireek described to you during the conversation in the tavern.

As long as the 🗑️ 0-0 **purple gemstone** is with you, your current weapon gains **+5** 🛡️ extra points in every battle.

You close the chest lid and stand up satisfied.

You can try to open the barred gate (#245).

You can start exploring the corridor (#152).

Or you can crawl back through the narrow and damp tunnel you came through (#33).

#362

You race through a narrow, winding street. To your right, you see the city wall.

The guards are hot on your heels.

You can go right from here (#246), forward (#15), or left (#53).

#363

You leave 📖**Dispel** and the kind hospitality behind to track down and find Kiena. You suspect she came further in this direction, and you enthusiastically step toward 📖**Moonward**.

The road stretches smoothly beneath your feet, but dusk sweeps in swiftly, cloaking the path in shadow, urging you to seek a campsite tucked away behind trees and tangled bushes. After a brief scout, you stumble upon a cozy hollow, an ideal nook for kindling a small campfire to roast your dinner. With practiced ease, you snare a wandering rabbit, swiftly skewering it over the flames, its savory aroma curling through the air, teasing your hunger as it sizzles to perfection.

You're just savoring the near-finished rabbit when odd rustles drift from the nearby undergrowth. At first, you dismiss them as nocturnal critters, but a creeping certainty tightens your chest — these sounds carry a deliberate weight, not the skitter of animals. The campfire's glow has drawn something — or someone — closer, and your first night promises to be anything but restful.

Abruptly, three figures burst from the bushes, their rough silhouettes marked by glinting steel and tattered cloaks — wandering bandits, no doubt lured by the beacon of your firelight, their eyes gleaming with intent in the flickering shadows.

It is sure now that they will give you a little workout before dinner.

Bandit #1 (with Sword)	8⚡1🌀 ☉4→∣←3🛡
Bandit #2 (with Sword)	6⚡2🌀 ☉5→∣←2🛡
Bandit #3 (with Dagger)	9⚡3🌀 ○2→∣←2🛡

If by any miracle you survive this fight against the three bandits (#110).

#364

You run down a narrow little street, the scent of the sea growing stronger, and you believe you can already see the masts from here. However, you can't see at all which path will take you to the harbor from here.

> If you have ♀a map of 🗺Whitpoint's secret streets with you, you can use it here by forming a two-digit number from the first and last digits, adding the third number, then adding the resulting value to this chapter's number, and continue the story there.

The guards are hot on your heels.

You can go left from here (#305), or right (#264).

#365

You walk through the opening and enter a chamber half submerged in water; as you suspected from the other chamber, there is indeed an altar on the wall, you see a few completely dried flower stems placed in front of the altar, surprisingly, the elements decorating the altar seem completely untouched. Faded in luster and woven with cobwebs, but it seems no one has yet felt the urge to steal the gemstones.

If you wish to examine the altar more closely (#100).

Or you can leave the chamber through either of the two exits, on one hand southeast (#17), or westward you see a water-covered chamber that might still be interesting (#186).

#366

"Kiena doesn't help anyone. Kiena is searching for the stones to destroy them," he replies to you, then retreats into his hut.

His answer didn't help much.

You can try to coax him out again (#70), or if you think it's time to return to the main road, you can leave this strange hut and its occupant behind (#50).

#367

Wandering in the dense forest, you spot a small campsite consisting of a few tents. You cautiously hide behind one of the bushes while you carefully observe how many there might be around. As far as their conversation filters over here, you figure out that not every one of the gang is here at the moment, only two, perhaps three of them might be present.

If you want to reveal yourself to them (#75).

If you decide instead that this is too risky and turn back (#50).

#368

You enter an empty chamber after a few steps, where apparently there is nothing.

If you have the 💡**map of the watchtower** with you, you can search here for the secret entrance to the underground dungeons by adding the two numbers and adding them to this chapter's number, then continue there.

If the dungeons don't interest you, you can go back to the chamber to the southwest through the iron-bound door (#263).

#369

The street leads to the riverbank, where you run parallel to the river until you reach a narrow bridge.

The guards are hot on your heels.

You can go right from here, across the bridge (#42), or left (#264).

#370

You step back and charge to push the door off its hinges with as much force as possible.

The door doesn't budge, and you awkwardly bounce back from the sturdy structure. You feel your shoulder strain; this attempt now costs you **-3⚡** points.

Perhaps brute force won't help here, but if you have a sword, you could try prying with it, maybe it will give (#227).

Alternatively, you can take a closer look at the stacked shelves on the opposite wall (#333).

Or you can leave the kitchen by crawling back through the small opening toward the corridor from where you originally came (#191).

#371

You're not too proud, but you certainly took part in the desecration of the altar.

However, now anyone can see that a small secret tunnel is hidden behind the altar.

You can crawl through the tunnel (#160).

Or you can leave the prayer chamber through the northern corridor (#101).

#372

You keep running down the main street, which sharply turns to the right. Suddenly, the salty scent of the sea hits your nose.

The guards are hot on your heels.

You can continue along the main street (#315); looking to your left, you see three narrower streets leading in different directions: you can take the left one (#310), the middle one (#68), or the right one (#335).

#373

"I am Nold Syanka, the wizard of the forest," he replies to you, then retreats into his hut.

His answer didn't help much.

You can try to coax him out again (#70), or if you think it's time to return to the main road, you can leave this strange hut and its occupant behind (#50).

#374

Your mind flashes back to the hidden cave system snaking toward the city's sewers — your secret shortcut. Heart racing, you plunge down the gorge's treacherous slope, boots skidding on loose gravel. A sudden slip sends you tumbling, but you lunge desperately, fingers clawing into a brittle bush that holds just long enough to arrest your fall, dangling precariously over the abyss.

However, you still get slightly injured, subtract **-2⚡** points from yourself.

Gasping, you scan the shadows and spot it: the cave mouth, cunningly veiled from the road above. You swing toward it, hauling yourself inside with a grunt. The passage squeezes tight, walls scraping your shoulders — no wonder the guards shun it, their lances useless in this claustrophobic choke. But it's secure, the path dipping steadily downward until the tunnel flares open, merging into the foul underbelly of the sewers.

Dank moisture slicks every surface, the reek of rot assaulting your nostrils as rats skitter through the gloom, their eyes glinting like tiny daggers. You press on, pulse thundering, until a grated manhole gleams ahead — unlocked!

You shove it upward with a metallic groan, thrusting your head into the blessed fresh air, gulping it down. Shock hits like a thunderclap: you're smack in the barracks' heart, the city gate looming mere feet away. Before you can blink, a bellow erupts — "Intruder!" A guard charges, sword drawn, boots pounding the earth. Adrenaline surges; you bolt from the hole, snatching up speed like a hunted hare, rabbit shoes forgotten in the frenzy.

This wasn't the stealthy entry into 📖**Whitpoint** you envisioned, but now it's a desperate sprint to the harbor, guards howling at your heels, praying to spot Kiena's ship — or any vessel ready to cast off and spirit you away.

Bursting through the gate, hope flickers; the labyrinthine streets twist like a serpent's coils ahead. You dodge into the chaos, weaving through startled crowds, heart hammering as you strain to lose your pursuers in the winding maze.

Entering through the city gate, your chances seem a bit better; you don't have much time to think, but at least on the tangled winding streets, you can try to shake off the guards.

You can run forward from here on the main street (#132), or sharply turn right onto a smaller street from here (#83), or sharply turn left onto another smaller street (#257).

#375

"Kiena doesn't help anyone. She found the stones at Hery Ruins and Miham Tower," he says, then retreats into his hut.

You received quite cryptic answers, but at least now you know where Kiena is headed next.

You can try to coax him out again (#70), or if you think it's time to return to the main road, you can leave this strange hut and its occupant behind (#50).

#376

You stand in a chamber dotted with small and large puddles, likely the central room of the underground dungeons, as far as you can tell. There's not much to see in the chamber, but there are a couple of exits from here.

The most striking is the barred gate on the northwest wall, which firmly blocks your path; however, beyond the bars, you glimpse what seems to be an old wine cellar, with several barrels still standing there, apparently untouched. The barred gate doesn't budge, and no matter how much you'd like to open it, you see no mechanism that would open the bars from here. It looks like this room can only be accessed from somewhere else.

From here, a staircase leads upward, obviously toward the exit from the underground chambers (#368).

On the northeast wall, you can enter another room (#3).

In contrast, to the southwest, two openings lead out: one opens from the far side of the chamber (#288), while the other leads somewhere through the nearer side (#175).

#377

You're running down the main street, there's no big crowd, and you easily keep your distance from your pursuers.

The guards are hot on your heels.

You can go left along the main street (#243), or right (#305), or forward where you see two small streets branching off in a Y shape; you can continue running along the left branch (#53), or even the right branch (#362).

#378

As you move through the short corridor, you likely reach the largest chamber of the granary.

The mud reaches up to your knees, making it quite difficult and unsteady to move. You stumble and stagger, it's a miracle you can keep your balance. Roll two dice, and if the resulting number is greater than your 🌀 points, subtract **-1**⚡ from yourself as you stumble in the mud and fall, sustaining a minor injury.

At this moment, the chamber has nothing but its four walls.

However, it has three exits, each leading to a longer or shorter corridor; you can continue through the shorter corridor to your left (#168), go along the branch leading to your right (#275), or even head in the third direction (#4).

#379

You reach for your weapon, but at that moment, some kind of lightning-like force strikes you, knocking you to the ground; for a short time, you can't feel your limbs and are unable to move. Subtract **-12⚡** points from yourself.

As you slowly start to come to and are able to move again, you stand up and dust yourself off.

You're somewhere in the middle of the forest, with no trace of the hut or the enigmatic hooded figure. Hesitantly, you start walking in one direction, hoping to find your way out from here (#324).

#380

The forest path leads straight into the village; you can't miss it, as the forest ends so abruptly that you suddenly find yourself on the main street. It's a lively little village, and you drop right into the midst of its everyday bustle, with everyone coming and going, seemingly doing something important.

You can head toward the marketplace and look around in the bustle there (#219).

You can pop into the tavern (#340).

You can follow the main road northwest, which leads out of the village (#118).

Or you can go northeast toward the golden wheat fields (#164).

Southward, you can leave the city through the forests (#347).

#381

"Do you need strength to win?" he asks, to which you nod.

> At that moment, some kind of lightning-like force strikes you, knocking you to the ground; for a short time, you can't feel your limbs and are unable to move. Subtract **-8 ⚡** points from yourself.

As you slowly start to come to and are able to move again, you stand up and dust yourself off. Whoever this mysterious figure was, they slightly strengthened one of your chosen weapons; add **+4 ⚔** points to it.

You're somewhere in the middle of the forest, with no trace of the hut or the enigmatic hooded figure. Hesitantly, you start walking in one direction, hoping to find your way out from here (#92).

#382

You nod smoothly, signaling your triumph, and with a deliberate motion, set a small pouch on the table, the purple gemstone nestled within. Knireek leans forward, his fingers deftly loosening the pouch's drawstring to peek inside; the gem's radiant glimmer catches his eye, and he swiftly cinches it shut.

His gaze meets yours, steady and sincere, as he unhooks a weighty pouch from his belt and slides it across the table. "Your payment for the gem, my friend," he says, voice warm with finality.

You gesture toward the leather glove, hoping for its return, but Knireek's companion fixes you with a stubborn stare, clearly unwilling to part with it. Knireek shakes his head gently, confirming you'll have to let it go — gold's your reward, the glove stays. Disappointment stings; you'd hoped for more from their honor, but a glance at their formidable trio quells any thought of protest — they're far too strong, each one alone a challenge, let alone all three together.

Don't forget that, you are selling the gem, and you'll no longer enjoy the gem's protective effect during battle.

You can accept the offered **20**✸ gold and walk out of the tavern (#143).

You can try to haggle and ask for more gold for your efforts (#35).

#383

The street leads to the riverbank, where you run parallel to the river until you reach a wide bridge.

The guards are hot on your heels.

You can go right from here, across the bridge (#42), forward (#342), or left back toward the main street (#132).

#384

Wandering in the dense forest, you see white flowers to your left.

You can go left from here (#237), or even forward (#286).

#385

The ogre greets you with a wide smile on his face, as if you were thousand-year-old friends, and from his kind words, you immediately feel at home here.

The forge hearth is glowing, and on one of the farther walls, at the table by the wall, you can see what useful things Youngrek makes here: mostly he forges tools, but as you see, a couple of sharp swords and weapons fit into his assortment.

Exactly what you might need in your search for Kiena.

You can buy weapons from him anytime, if you have enough gold with you.

You can buy from him 🧺 →|← the **basic knife** and dagger, ◯2→|←2🛡, for **8**⊛.

You can buy from him 🧺 →|← the **ornate knife** and dagger, ◯3→|←2🛡, for **10**⊛.

You can buy from him 🧺 →|← the **short sword** and shield, ⊙6→|←5🛡, for **17**⊛.

You can buy from him 🧺 →|← the **reinforced sword** and shield, ⊙9→|←6🛡, for **21**⊛.

You can buy from him 🧺 →|← the **hunter's bow** and arrows, ◎4→|←2🛡, for **26**⊛.

You can buy from him 🧺 →|← the **double-strung bow** and arrows, ◎5→|←3🛡 for **30**⊛.

Alternatively, you can ask him for advice on how to use your chosen weapon most effectively (#125).

But if you're ready to go, then through the paths behind the houses, you can head back toward the harbor in the direction of the fish market (#320), or following the city walls toward Wamake Gate (#140), or you can follow the signpost toward 🗺**Oceastall** northwest (#99), or toward **📖Moonward** southeast (#363), leaving **📖Dispel** completely behind you.

#386

The door opens silently, and you find yourself in a sort of smoking room; you can smell the heavy scent of smoke ingrained in the walls, curtains, and carpet. Beyond that, the room's decor is impeccable, with several portraits hanging on the walls and a highly detailed map of the empire, mainly depicting the roads running through it. You recognize almost all the major cities marked on it.

You hear noises and voices from upstairs; you are not alone in the house! Roll two dice; if the result is greater than your 𝓃 points, unfortunately, you failed to stay unnoticed and quiet; continue the story here (#13).

Three doors lead out of this room: one to the left (#154), another to the right (#250), but you can also choose the third door (#52).

If you already feel it's time to leave the house, you can do so from here through the garden (#145).

#387

The long narrow road ends abruptly in a short dead-end street, where, from the sign of one of the cottages, you deduce that some kind of healer might live here.

You can knock on the house if you wish (#228).

Or you can turn back from here, where after a few houses the street splits in two; you can choose the narrow little street leading south (#276), or head toward the slightly louder rumble, southwest from here (#107).

#388

The ladder is indeed old, and one or two rungs are already missing, but it perfectly supports your weight, so you comfortably climb down into an underground room, which immediately turns out to have been some kind of small wine cellar, judging from the barrels still standing here — some of them seem completely untouched.

You tap the side, and it indeed seems that there is still some liquid in them; the quality might be questionable, but definitely more than half full in one or two barrels.

Your curiosity won't leave you alone; good wine only gets better as it ages, so you carefully open one and even more carefully sniff it. To your surprise, the wine has a divine aroma; if the taste is only half as good, then you've found some kind of heavenly treasure here.

You tilt the barrel to drip a little through the bung hole, carefully splash it onto your palm, sniff it again, and then gulp down the few drops that didn't spill through your fingers. As expected, the wine has perfectly matured; this could even hold its place on kings' tables. It's a shame that this will never make it to a king's table from here — at least not by your doing.

However, if you have a 🧺**flask filled with water** from earlier, you can now replace its contents with this fine wine and take it with you. If you do so, note for yourself that this wine will mean **+6⚡** points when you decide to drink it.

Beyond the wine barrels, there's not much else to see; on the southwest wall, you see a barred gate without a lock, behind which is a larger room with small and large puddles here and there, and several smaller passages that might lead to more interesting places.

> If you have 💡**the map**, it can help you figure out how to open the barred gate by multiplying the two numbers and subtracting from this chapter's number, then continue there.

If you don't want to bother with the barred door, you can climb back up the ladder to the small pantry room above you at any time (#300).

#389

Since you came to rest, you lie down on the nomad bed, which is far less comfortable than it first appears, as if you were sleeping on uneven ground filled with small and large bumpy stones. You don't really find it comfortable, so after some tossing and turning, you give up the attempt.

You decide you can rest later, especially if you find Kiena.

Instead, you walk back down the stairs to the ground floor and throw yourself into the noisy bustle of the tavern (#5).

#390

With a flourish, Elliniar brandishes an exquisitely crafted bow, its sleek curves and taut string gleaming under the sunlight, paired with a quiver of arrows fletched in vibrant hues. It's a breathtaking masterpiece, its artistry leaping out even to your untrained eye. Beaming with pride, Elliniar declares he personally tests every bow, and this — this is his finest creation yet, a marvel of precision.

You grasp the bow, its featherlight frame almost dancing in your hands, and draw the string with a thrill coursing through you; it balances flawlessly, as if crafted from air itself, far lighter than any traditional bow, begging to be loosed at a target with exhilarating ease.

If you want to buy this splendid weapon from him, perhaps you can haggle (#293).

You can ask him about Kiena too if you haven't already (#298).

Or you can thank him for the friendly demonstration and set off on your way. A path leads north from here (#156), or you can go west following the city wall (#356).

#391

You climb up the stairs until you reach the ladder, and from there to the manhole.

You cautiously peer out from behind the sewer grates to check if the coast is clear, and when you hear no noises nearby, you quickly climb back up to the street. You slide the manhole cover back into place, so practically no one could tell where you came from.

You bypass the tents, and here you're back in familiar territory by the river (#60).

#392

You claim your spot at the stern, heart pounding with anticipation as Captain Rottora's crew hauls the final crates aboard, their grunts echoing over the creaking deck before slamming them into the hold. With a sharp whistle, Rottora signals departure — the mooring ropes snap free, and the massive hull lurches to life, groaning against the waves like a awakening beast. It's official: you're bidding farewell to 📖**Dispel's** warm embrace, perhaps for ages, as the ship surges into the unknown.

The oarsmen strain with furious strokes, muscles bulging under the strain at the river's mouth where it spills into the churning sea, battling the relentless current in a sweat-drenched showdown. But upstream, the fight eases, the vessel slicing through the water with gathering momentum — though laden to the brim, it glides like a predator on the prowl. Hours stretch into a mesmerizing vigil: you scan the lush riverside, where vibrant foliage rustles with hidden wildlife, birds exploding from the canopy in bursts of color, and the sun dips low, painting the horizon in fiery strokes.

Yet tranquility reigns all day, a deceptive calm that builds an undercurrent of tension — until night crashes down like a velvet curtain. Rottora steers toward a broad bank, dropping anchor with a resonant splash; "No fool tempts the river after dark," he growls, tales of wrecked ships and ghostly shoals hanging in the air like a curse.

Shore-bound flames leap to life as the crew kindles a roaring fire, skewering a plump wild boar that sizzles and spits, its heavenly aroma twisting your gut with ravenous hunger. You devour the feast, vitality surging through you — gaining **+4⚡** health points — as laughter and stories swirl amid the crackling blaze.

Opting for solid ground over the ship's endless sway, you confide in Rottora your need for a steady night's rest after twelve rocking ordeals at sea. He nods grimly: "Camp by the fire if you must, but stay sharp — shadows hide teeth."

The night's first watch slips by in fitful dozes, your senses attuned to the deal you struck for passage, when suddenly — rustles erupt into a cacophony, branches snapping like bones.

In a heartbeat, three shadowy figures burst from the undergrowth, blades glinting wickedly in the firelight — roving bandits, drawn like moths to the blaze or the savory smoke, their snarls promising violence as they charge with murderous glee!

Time to earn your passage.

Bandit #1 (with Bow)	8 ⚡3 🗡 ◉5 →|← 1 🛡
Bandit #2 (with Sword)	6 ⚡2 🗡 ◉5 →|← 4 🛡
Bandit #3 (with Dagger)	9 ⚡1 🗡 ○2 →|← 2 🛡

If by any miracle you survive this fight against the three bandits (#27).

#393

You mention Kiena's name, and two shake their heads, but the third lumberjack has visibly heard this name before, and sizes you up somewhat suspiciously.

He asks why you're looking for her.

You can lie to him that you owe her a few gold coins and would like to repay it (#204), or you can tell the truth that you're on the trail of the stones, and Kiena will surely be able to help find them (#174).

#394

You take a few steps down the main street, then slow down and look around thoughtfully, deciding where to continue.

You can head toward the marketplace, perhaps finding something interesting there (#219).

Or you can walk south along the road, leaving the city behind through the forest path (#347).

You can turn off the main street toward the wheat fields from here (#164).

Or you can follow the main road northwest and leave the city that way (#118).

You can also enter the tavern from here (#340).

#395

You find two groups noteworthy; one group is obviously some kind of local lumberjacks, at least judging by their attire, and they are peacefully drinking wine; the other group is a much grumpier congregation, among them you find the scarred face the most intriguing.

You have little to lose; you can sit down and try to talk with the lumberjacks (#344), or you can choose the company of the scarred ones (#232).

Or if neither group appeals to you, you can even talk to the innkeeper (#281).

#396

You enter a larger chamber, where a long dining table surrounded by chairs stands against the southeast wall. There is still food on the table, but from what you can see from a safe distance, flies or gnats are already swarming in small clouds around it.

This was obviously a dining room, but since the tower became a haunted place, it clearly hasn't been used.

The chamber has two exits: one leads northeast (#263), and the other continues through a narrower corridor on the wall opposite the dining table (#191).

But before you leave, you can take a closer look at the table, despite the flies and gnats (#112).

#397

You step to the table, where you can only confidently identify a few items among the tools. If you want to buy something, the following might be useful:

You can buy a 🛒 **shovel** here for **3**⊛.

You can buy a 🛒 **rasp** here for **2**⊛.

You can buy a 🛒 ⊶ **sharpening stone** here for **1**⊛, and as long as the sharpening stone is with you, you gain **+1→|←** point during fighting.

Once you've finished shopping, just walk back to the street (#77).

#398

You press your weight against the coffin's heavy stone lid, muscles straining as you nudge it aside with determined heaves, the slab grinding reluctantly until a narrow gap opens, just wide enough to slip one hand inside.

The effort leaves you breathless, a bead of sweat trickling down — lose **1⚡** point. But the coffin's secrets beckon; peering into the dim interior yields little, shadows swallowing the scant light filtering through.

Undeterred, you reach in, fingers brushing dry bones clad in brittle armor — a warrior's remains, untouched for weeks, perhaps years. Your hand grazes the cold edge of a blade, tracing cautiously to its hilt. With careful tugs, you ease the sword free through the tight opening, its form emerging into the faint glow.

The weapon gleams with a row of tiny, glinting gemstones embedded along its blade, the hilt molding perfectly to your grip, whispering of a warrior's legacy. As you wield it, a strange, tingling surge of magic pulses through you, an eerie sensation as if you could command the dead themselves — its source and meaning eluding you in the crypt's heavy silence.

In any case, you can take this 🛒 →|← **sword inlaid with red gemstones (3-51)**, ⊙**9**→|←**4🛡**, and this sword has a 🛒 ◖◗ **magical bone extension** will gift you an additional ◖◗**+5**→|←**+2🛡** advantage, if you fight against skeletons.

You won't find much else here, but if you haven't done so yet, you can look at the crests on the wall (#221) or even leave the small burial chamber the way you came (#45).

#399

You prepare yourself mentally to try opening the barred door by pulling it toward you without a key. With great force, you grab the bars and yank; you don't expect the hinges embedded in the wall holding the bars to give way so easily.

The entire grate, as it is, rips out of the wall completely, so effortlessly that you lose your balance, fall backward, and with that momentum, pull the whole heavy iron structure onto yourself.

> It all happens so suddenly that you can't even collect yourself before it's over; you feel mild pain in your chest, you can deduct **-3**⚡ points from yourself for this sudden action, but either way, at least you've cleared the path.

You crawl out from under the bars and carefully lay them down in the corridor as space allows, so next time it won't block your path.

From here, you can now go in three directions.

You can explore the corridor behind the freshly opened recess heading south (#101).

You can continue east along this branch (#198).

You can go west back toward the statue (#239).

#400

Who could have foreseen that a humble garden gate, tucked amid blooming vines and whispering foliage, would unveil a secret artery — a winding cobblestone path slicing through the shadows, delivering you straight to the bustling heart of the harbor! With the guards' frantic shouts fading into echoes behind you, triumph surges through your veins as you saunter among the majestic ships, their masts piercing the twilight sky like spears of fate. You query captains and crew alike, voice steady amid the salty spray and creaking timbers: which vessel departs at dawn's first light? And does any soul here know the elusive Kiena?

Amid the throng, a shadowy figure emerges — Captain Nekor, his weathered face etched with rogue's cunning and eyes gleaming like storm-tossed waves. He leans in, breath laced with rum and secrets, confessing that Kiena's name dances on the winds he's chased. "I know her course," he rasps, "and for a fat purse of gold, I'll veer my sails toward Hery Ruins, where she races ahead. For you — and that glittering bounty — I'll bend the seas themselves!"

With no grander path unfolding, destiny's hand compels you: you seal the pact, coins clinking like the toll of adventure as you hand over the gold. Nekor's laughter booms like thunder, welcoming you aboard the infamous Worn Dogs, her scorched hull a testament to battles won and tempests defied. "Bunk with the crew, mate," he chuckles, "for the first officer's quarters belong to another — our mystery guest. High tide swells; the moment they board, we cast off into the abyss!"

Your queries about this enigmatic traveler yield only cryptic grins, but a thrilling intuition ignites within: could it be Kiena herself, veiled in the captain's silence? As the ship groans to life beneath your feet, sails unfurling like wings of legend, the harbor lights dwindle to stars on the horizon. The open sea beckons, vast and untamed, promising revelations amid crashing waves and endless skies. And so, under the watchful gaze of the moon, your epic quest hurtles toward its fateful crescendo... while sailing these treacherous waters, the truth shall unfurl at last!

⇨ **To be continued...**

My friend!

✺ Congratulations on finishing this story!

I suspect I didn't make your journey easy with all the clever and clumsy traps I set to slow you down, but I hope that whichever strategy you ultimately chose — to catch this ship and presumably Kiena on it — brought you many pleasant hours of exciting gameplay and reading.

And I have a good new for you that the story does not end here.

This is just the beginning of a great story.

Kiena will be back in **Bonding Kiena**.

Printed in Dunstable, United Kingdom

70018158R00170